Dear Reader,

My husband
and after all
what I expected.
Instead, what struck me was the proliferation of
great coffeehouses. I couldn't help thinking that
Seattle would be the perfect home for a caffeine
junkie, and soon my heroine, Sheryl Dayton, was
born. She began telling me all about herself and
her problems (when you're a writer, conversations
with imaginary people are normal and don't
require medication). Luckily for Sheryl and me,
Harlequin announced a new comedy line—
Harlequin Flipside, the perfect home for my
caffeine addict who might sound sarcastic at
times but is intensely loyal to friends and family.

It's that very sense of loyalty that brings Sheryl
into conflict with journalist Nathan Hall, whose
columns question the integrity of Sheryl's friend
and employer. Sheryl is prepared to dislike
Nathan on sight after his accusatory newspaper
pieces, but she doesn't count on him making
her laugh or having eyes as rich and dark as
her favorite espresso.

A lifelong fan of romantic comedy, I'm very
excited to be writing one of the launch books
for Harlequin Flipside and hope that Sheryl
and Nathan give you plenty of reasons to smile
as they overcome the obstacles between them
and fall in love.

Happy holidays,

Tanya Michaels

"Did you just invite me to dinner?"

Nathan widened his smile. "Sounded like it, didn't it?"

Well, Sheryl was going to say no, of course. How completely out of her mind would she have to be to say anything else?

But before common sense could assert itself, she nodded. "Sounds good." When she got home tonight, she'd have to check herself into some twelve-step program for women who made unwise romantic decisions.

Not necessarily unwise, the devil on her shoulder insisted. Maybe dinner with Nathan could be excused with the same principle she always used when dieting—have some extra chocolate before the day started to get cravings out of the way.

"You in the mood for anything?" he asked.

"Wh-whatever restaurant you like is fine," she was relieved to hear herself say. Because saying, "You and a bottle of chocolate syrup" might have been inappropriate. Not to mention the mess it would've made of her bedsheets.

"Who Needs Decaf?"

Tanya Michaels

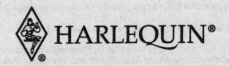

HARLEQUIN®

TORONTO • NEW YORK • LONDON
AMSTERDAM • PARIS • SYDNEY • HAMBURG
STOCKHOLM • ATHENS • TOKYO • MILAN • MADRID
PRAGUE • WARSAW • BUDAPEST • AUCKLAND

With special thanks to Anna DeStefano,
Jenni Grizzle and Maureen Hardegree
for your candor, insight and encouragement.

And, as always, thank you, Jarrad.
What would I do without you?

ISBN 0-373-44180-0

WHO NEEDS DECAF?

ABOUT THE AUTHOR

Tanya Michaels has been reading books all her life, and romances have always been her favorite. She is thrilled to be writing for Harlequin—and even more thrilled that the stories she makes up now qualify as "work" and exempt her from doing the dishes after dinner. The 2001 Maggie Award winner lives in Georgia with her two wonderful children and a loving husband whose displays of support include reminding her to quit writing and eat something. Thankfully, between her husband's thoughtfulness and that stash of chocolate she keeps at her desk, Tanya can continue writing her books in no danger of wasting away.

For more information on Tanya, her upcoming releases and periodic giveaways, please visit her Web site at www.mindspring.com/~tjmic.

Books by Tanya Michaels

HARLEQUIN DUETS
96—THE MAID OF DISHONOR

Dear Reader,

A brand-new year is around the corner and once the holiday celebrations are over, it's time to make resolutions. And this time, ignore those pesky ones you never really pay attention to! Instead, make sure to give yourself a break from your troubles. Relax and unwind—with a Harlequin Flipside novel! These clever and witty stories blend comedy and romance in a way that's sure to smooth away any tension....

In December, award-winning author Jill Shalvis brings us *Natural Blond Instincts*, a story about an independent woman who finally has the chance to prove to her conservative family that she can succeed in the family business. Of course, the gorgeous man who shares her position is so distracting she's having trouble focusing on the job!

We also have *Who Needs Decaf?* by Tanya Michaels. Given the stress of her life, this PR exec needs large injections of high-octane java to get through her day. Too bad the caffeine isn't having an effect on her love life. At least, not before she meets the good-looking guy who's determined to dig up dirt on her company....

Look for two new Harlequin Flipside novels every month at your favorite bookstore. And be sure to check us out online at www.harlequinflipside.com.

Have a Happy New Year and enjoy!

Wanda Ottewell
Editor

Mary-Theresa Hussey
Executive Editor

1

STEERING HER COMPACT CAR onto the exit ramp off Seattle's Interstate 90, Sheryl Dayton frowned, and not just because of the possibility of ice on the road. Had her car made a noise when she turned? A kind of *thwacka thwacka thwacka?*

Not now, please. This really isn't a good time. Funds were always tighter coming into December, but holiday season aside, Sheryl was trying to save up to buy her own place. Not to mention that with the escalating situation at work, she had no time in her busy schedule to visit a mechanic.

Deciding tough love was her best immediate course of action, she inhaled sharply and threatened the car. "Don't even think about breaking down until after the first of the year. If you do, I'll yank your spark plugs out with my bare hands and hang them on my Christmas tree!" She was only marginally sure she'd know what a spark plug was if she saw one—public relations was her specialty, not the inner workings of American automobiles—but she did know how to solve the disturbing *thwacka-thwacka-thwacka* problem.

Sheryl turned up the radio.

An elaborate musical introduction swelled through the speakers, followed by the voice of an enthusiastic singer confiding that her true love had gifted her with a partridge and a pear tree. Sheryl didn't have a true love, herself, but she *did* have an ex-boyfriend. Brad Hammond, owner of Hammond Gaming Software, the company Sheryl worked for.

On the first day of Christmas, my ex-boyfriend gave to me, a good job and a migraine.

When she'd broken things off with Brad six months ago, Sheryl had worried it would be too awkward to continue running the miniscule public relations department at Hammond, but Brad had implored her to stay, insisting he needed her. Which had proven to be prophetic.

Until now, Sheryl had devoted her time and energy to gaining favorable public attention for the up-and-coming software company, but their spot in the limelight had backfired on them when a Web site owner filed a lawsuit claiming theft of intellectual property. With revived public interest in Tolkien, along with some recent, popular fantasy novels and movies, HGS's newly released fantasy-action game, *Xandria Quest,* had promised to be their first major success. But writer Kendra Mathers was claiming that the premise, characters and·levels for the game had been stolen from her online epic fantasy story. Sheryl's publicity skills were suddenly needed for damage control.

"Particularly," she muttered, "since Nathan Hall seems intent on causing damage."

The columnist for the *Seattle Sojourner* had written a couple of pieces on the pending suit, and his writing made Sheryl nervous. He managed to blend cynicism and passion in his annoyingly factual columns—she'd scanned carefully for glaring, malicious, libelous errors. Nathan Hall resonated with readers, and Sheryl worried about his insinuations that big bad Brad Hammond, "overnight success," was now sticking it to the little guys he'd so recently been one of.

Sheryl snorted indelicately as she approached the parking garage of the modestly sized, yet state-of-the-art building HGS leased. *Big bad Brad Hammond, indeed.* When she and Brad had watched the *Titanic* DVD together, he'd wept like a baby, and she'd spent the better part of an hour trying to console him.

That one evening, she realized now, had encapsulated their relationship. Though a good-looking programming phenom, well on his way to becoming a rich man, Brad was a little too needy in other ways, almost painfully earnest for a man who owned a company in a fiercely competitive field. But Sheryl doubted it would be a good PR spin to release an announcement that her boss was too naive to steal from anyone.

Maybe as a last resort.

In her opinion, she and HGS's attorney, Mark Campbell, had sent out some brilliant press releases, but she noted that the *Sojourner* hadn't bothered to print any of them. Brad praised her work, but refused to worry much about the problem since, as he saw it, *Xandria Quest* was his baby and he hadn't stolen it from anyone.

Rolling down her window, Sheryl smiled at the parking garage attendant who sat in the small booth, his gloved hands cradling a steaming thermos of coffee. The rich aroma made her glance longingly at her own to-go container. She hadn't allowed herself to lift it from the safety of its snug cup holder as she drove on the freeway, for fear of spilling burning liquid down the front of her ivory knit tunic and skirt.

"Morning, Henry."

The man's weathered face wrinkled into an answering smile as he tipped his uniform cap. "Ms. Dayton," he returned, despite all the times she'd asked him to call her Sheryl. "Say, is your car acting up? Thought I heard sort of a *thumba thumba thumba* as you came round the corner."

"'Thumba,' huh? Nope, no 'thumba' here." Her response didn't stem *completely* from denial. No way was the sound more of a *thumba* than a *thwacka*.

"Oh, okay. Well, I'm glad," Henry said. "I'd hate to see a nice lady like you get stranded on the side of a cold road at night, after the late evenings you put in here."

Well, when you looked at it that way... *Note to self— call mechanic on lunch break, do not end up freeway Popsicle.*

He held up a folded edition of Wednesday's paper. "You seen the *Sojourner?* Your boss made headlines again."

Surely, with approximately two and a half million people in the metro Seattle area, reporters could find something to write about besides her boss! What new angle could Hall possibly have used for his latest piece when the case was still in the early deposition stages? Sheryl decided that along with the Christmas check she'd planned to give Henry as his annual tip, she'd also throw in a subscription to the *Post-Intelligencer* or *Seattle Times.*

Forcing a pleasant tone, she said, "Have a nice day, Henry."

"You, too, Ms. Dayton."

Too late for that, but she nodded anyway as she pulled her car up the entrance ramp.

In the elevator from the garage to the main lobby, Sheryl sipped her white-chocolate cappuccino and dreaded the day. Or more accurately, the fallout from Tuesday evening, which was when Brad saw his therapist each week. Brad had read somewhere that top-level executives needed balance more than anyone since so many people depended on them, and he'd gone right out and hired a shrink. Unfortunately, the quack dictated Brad and Sheryl must have a long conversation to determine *exactly* where they'd gone wrong, so Brad could learn and grow as a "giving, loving being" and be more successful in all future relationships.

Well, he would have to learn and grow on his own time, not Sheryl's. Their relationship was strictly professional now.

The elevator dinged and the doors parted, allowing Sheryl to step into the reception area she knew so well. When they'd moved into this building from the tiny space HGS had occupied before, Sheryl and her roommate, Meka, an interior decorator, had helped Brad pick out the furnishings. Right down to the blue leather upholstered chair the plump receptionist, Denise Avery, was currently standing on.

"Morning," Denise said from around the thumbtacks clenched between her lips.

In her hands the receptionist held a shiny red-and-green garland that she was pinning onto the wall in one remaining bare corner of the room. Clearly in the spirit of the season, Denise looked adorably younger than her almost-forty years in a red jumper and green sweater, a piece of plastic ivy tucked into her bouncy blond ponytail. Her festive mood was also evident in the pot of poinsettias sitting on the small rectangular coffee table and the fake snow that adorned the window of the executive conference room.

"Brad asked for you to report to his office immediately," the receptionist continued before Sheryl could voice a greeting. "Unless, of course, you haven't had coffee yet, in which case see him immediately after your stop to the breakroom."

Sheryl grinned and held up the fortifying cappuccino. Her favorite thing about this city, a caffeine-addict's nirvana, was that no street corner was without either a Starbucks or Seattle's Best Coffee. She'd had two cups of coffee at home, naturally, but that was to get her through personal grooming and the drive to the office. Each day, she needed at least one cup post-drive, and then she was good to go until afternoon fatigue set in. Woe to anyone who encountered her on a morning she didn't get that crucial third cup.

Her grin faded as she considered Denise's announcement. Brad wanted to see her immediately? What an uncommonly executive order...unless he wanted to once again try to convince her to rehash each second of their brief, passionless relationship. "Did he say why he wanted me?"

"Nathan Hall," Denise replied, an edge to her chirpy voice.

Exasperated, Sheryl ran a hand through her shoulder-length hair. "Right." She'd temporarily pushed aside Henry's comment about a new story. "I'm just going to make a quick stop in the breakroom and see if there's a copy of this morning's *Sojourner*." She personally didn't want to buy a copy and give the paper her money, but she should read the latest piece so that she knew what she was up against.

As she headed down the carpeted corridor, Sheryl thought to herself that there was at least one Hall she might like to deck.

WEDNESDAY EVENING, Sheryl unknotted the belt at her waist, then threw her overcoat onto the buttery soft sectional sofa with a vengeance that was probably unfair to both jacket and couch. *"Argh!"*

Inside the kitchen adjacent to the living room, Tameka Williams glanced up from the island countertop where she was chopping carrots. Her thin, elegant eyebrows arched over teasing hazel eyes. "Bad day at the office, dear?"

Despite her mood, Sheryl laughed. Her best friend often had that effect. Sheryl couldn't think of anyone in the state of Washington who'd make a better roommate than Meka, but after growing up in a big family and having roommates since her freshman year of college, Sheryl was ready to be alone. Especially now that Meka and Tyler McAfee were practically engaged, often unintentionally making Sheryl a third wheel in her own apartment.

Abandoning her demiboots, Sheryl padded in stocking feet to the kitchen. "I don't know which of them is driving me crazier—the Columnist who Stole Christmas, or the Boyfriend of Christmas Past who's haunting me."

"Okay, the boyfriend is a certain blond software genius who gets weepy after Leonardo DiCaprio films, right? And the reporter would be...what's his name? Nate?"

"Nathan. Hall. My nemesis. I get paid to make the company look good, and this jerk seems determined to paint us as evil."

"Evil sells papers," Meka said with a shrug of her graceful shoulders. Everything about Meka was graceful, and she looked absurdly elegant in a red-velour two-piece lounging set.

Opening the refrigerator, Sheryl hunted for a bottle of wine. After the day she'd had, she could use a glass. Unfortunately the closest thing they had was the cooking sherry Meka had pulled out to use for dinner. Still, Sheryl stared hard at the fridge's interior for a moment, as though she could summon a nice Chardonnay through sheer willpower.

"I saw that piece he wrote today," Meka continued. "He made some good points, about why does society reward wrongdoing? You guys have been accused of basically stealing *Xandria Quest*, yet sales are actually up for the game right now, making—"

Abandoning the attempted Chardonnay telepathy, Sheryl whirled around. "Reward wrongdoing? We didn't *do* anything wrong!"

And sales might be up in the short run, but Sheryl was worried about the long-term results. If this case actually went to court and they lost... People in the industry had predicted Hammond Gaming Software would be the Next Big Thing, but the company wasn't big yet and couldn't afford any substantial financial setbacks. Or a damaged reputation.

Dropping her knife, Meka held up both hands in an I-surrender pose. "You're right, I'm sorry. I am on your side. He's just very persuasive."

"I know." Sheryl narrowed her eyes. "That's what bothers me about him—his talent. He doesn't sensationalize, he's careful to use the right words like *alleged*, but it's not those words that stick with you, it's the overall impression. The impression that he's a man of integrity on the side of justice."

"You sound almost admiring."

"Hardly!" Sheryl poured herself some apple juice, deciding to pretend it was hard cider. "It's just that it would be easier to get the public to hear our side if Hall didn't seem so damned credible. *We're* the victims here!"

"Not to change the subject from the nemesis you're all fired-up about while we're in a room full of sharp utensils or anything, but what's Brad doing that's making you crazy?"

"Two things. One, he asked me to go on a date."

"Oh, no!" An expression of amused horror settled across Meka's pretty mocha-colored features. "Don't tell me that incompetent shrink of his convinced Brad he can win you back."

Laughing, Sheryl clarified, "You don't understand, he wants me to go along on his date with another woman."

"Didn't think our man Brad had it in him to be kinky."

Another laugh, this time with the unpleasant side effect of choking on apple juice. "He wants me to try to spot possible trouble areas in the relationship. He says it's the least I can do since I won't commit a few hours of rehashing *our* relationship. I told him this prospective new relationship wouldn't go anywhere if he brought along an ex to chaperone."

"For a boy who's such a genius in *some* areas..."

"Tell me about it."

"So what's the second thing?"

Sheryl's fingers tightened, and she was glad the glass in her hand was actually made from shatterproof plastic. "He wants us to extend an olive branch to Nathan Hall."

Reaching for a bag of russet potatoes, Meka froze, blinking. "You're the relations expert, but isn't that just begging for mercy and making yourselves look weak?''

"Trust me, I'm not happy about it."

Gritting her teeth, Sheryl recalled her meeting that morning with Brad. He'd asked her to personally deliver the latest press release in case the *Sojourner* wanted to use it—though history had proven that unlikely—and, as HGS's official publicity representative, let Hall know that Brad was readily available for comment and welcomed Nathan's questions. She'd tried to get Brad to reconsider or at least get their attorney's opinion, but Brad had insisted the attorney worked for him, not the other way around.

She'd suggested Brad actually send their attorney on this errand, but her boss had felt a six-five man who spoke in stern legalese didn't promote the friendly, accessible image he wanted to convey. Also, Brad had seemed to think that sending a lawyer to see the man who'd been writing carefully derogatory articles about him was an implied threat of some sort.

Sheryl could usually cajole Brad into seeing her point, but he was being strangely stubborn about this. Was it just because he hated the thought of being disliked by someone? Especially someone with a loyal readership.

With a sigh, she told Meka, "I'm afraid Brad half believes it's as simple as convincing Mr. Hall what swell folks we are, then he'll stop writing those mean articles and the whole mess will go away."

"First, swell folks make boring headlines." Meka enumerated her observations on her fingers. "Second, even if the columns stop, Brad still has the lawsuit to deal with. Third, Nathan may view your 'olive branch' as sucking up to get him to stop and become even more self-righteous."

Sheryl settled herself on one of the two soft-covered stools that sat at the raspberry-colored breakfast counter. Decorated in raspberry and cream with soft lighting and an almost-view of the Space Needle, the kitchen was so inviting that she and Meka had most of their conversations here even though the living room furniture was expensive and comfy, while the kitchen bar stools eventually put one's butt to sleep.

"All good points," Sheryl agreed with her roommate. "Points I tried to make earlier today. Three hundred and sixty-four days a year, he's Mister Mellow, letting his savvy staff advise him on what to do—which is what he pays us for—but then there's that one other day, out there lurking..."

"And today was that day?" When Sheryl didn't answer, Meka added, "Too bad Nathan Hall isn't one of those columnists with a picture next to his byline. Then we'd have something to blow up and throw darts at."

Sheryl had never thought about what the journalist looked like, but it wasn't hard to imagine him as green and hairy, à la a certain, bitter Seuss character bent on sucking the joy out of the holiday season for others. Draining her glass, she decided that pretend hard cider wasn't cutting it. What she really needed was a vacation, but since that was out of the question...

"Meka, what are your plans for the weekend? It's been a while since we had a really good girls' night out."

Her roommate stared down, seeming oddly intent on making eye contact with the potatoes. "You're right, it *has* been too long, but this isn't a good weekend. I'm sorry, but Tyler and I—"

"You don't have to sound contrite." Sheryl forced a smile for her friend's benefit despite a small pang of disappointment. "He is your boyfriend."

"I know, but you're just as important and I feel like we've barely spent any time together the last few months. I'd cancel, but Ty's parents are coming into town this weekend and he's asked me to meet them Saturday."

Sheryl let out a low whistle. She couldn't remember the last relationship she'd been in where she'd reached the meet-the-parents stage. Of course, not everyone's parents lived as close to their children as hers. "Meeting the parents."

"Yeah. In a word, *yikes.* I'm terrified already, and it's still days away. You and I could go out Friday night, but I wouldn't be any fun."

"Besides, it would probably be better not to show up hungover on Saturday," Sheryl teased, even though neither of them were hardcore party drinkers.

"Well, I promise you that we'll do a girls' night soon," Meka said, her smile grateful. "In the meantime, I can at least offer dinner. Some comfort food to take the edge off your day?"

Though Sheryl quickly accepted the offer of her roommate's gourmet cooking, she chose to look at it not as comfort food, but as the traditional feast soldiers of old enjoyed the night before battle. Tomorrow, she faced Nathan Hall.

SHERYL STOOD in a lobby full of modern art sculptures, waiting for one of four elevators to open and take her to the floor that housed the *Sojourner's* staff offices. She hadn't scheduled an appointment, merely called to ask what time Nathan was expected in today. Sheryl wanted to have the element of surprise, not give the journalist an opportunity to devise questions so pointed, she couldn't possibly answer them safely. And, of course, not answering a question only made a person look guilty.

With an impatient glance, she assessed her distorted reflection in the mirrored elevator doors. Meka had suggested that her navy blue cashmere sweater over a well-tailored calf-length skirt would be feminine enough to keep her from seeming combative, while the dark colors said "take me seriously." Not wanting to look girly, Sheryl had neither applied much makeup nor curled her hair. She'd stuck to the basics around her green eyes, applied some lipstick and just brushed her brown hair until the natural red highlights shone. *Cosmo* wouldn't be calling to ask her to cover-model any time soon, but she looked good enough for this meeting.

A small beep sounded and a light glowed above the elevator to her right. She moved toward it, but a slight masculine chuckle behind her stopped her.

Turning, Sheryl located the owner of that low chuckle—a man much taller than she, probably even taller than Meka. He wore a brown leather jacket over a Sonics sweatshirt—both of which merely seemed like adornments for his broad shoulders—and jeans of indeterminable age. The dark denim didn't look worn or faded, but the pants molded to the man's lower body well enough to give the impression that they were comfortably broken-in.

Berating herself for staring at his rather promising lower body, Sheryl jerked her head up and fell into eyes the same rich brown color as his hair. His entire appearance made her think of things hot and delicious. Chocolate, coffee, dark caramels melting...

"That one's broken," he said, angling his chin toward the elevator she'd approached. "It lights up, but only goes down. No idea why maintenance still hasn't fixed it, but the only place it will take you is underground parking."

The elevator to her left lit and opened, and she instinctively stepped aside for the people exiting. Then she entered the empty conveyance, and the man with the espresso eyes joined her, his clean, soapy scent a relief in the overly perfumed air left by the elevator's last passengers.

He reached for the number panel the same time she did, and their hands brushed. Both of them stilled, but neither moved away, so the contact and the strange humming it stirred in Sheryl's blood continued.

Finally, she pulled her hand back, saying softly, "Five, please."

The man stared for a moment as though he were going to ask, "Five what?", but then he nodded with a self-conscious laugh. "Oh. Five, right."

Sheryl bit the inside of her lip to keep from smiling. If it had taken him a moment to realize she was talking about which floor she wanted, then she hadn't been the only one affected by their shared, electric touch. Had she ever had such an immediate reaction to a man?

He belatedly processed her request and hit Five, but when he didn't select a button for himself, Sheryl lost her struggle with the suppressed smile. "Um, don't you want to hit a button for your floor?" she reminded him gently. Wow, maybe she really had rattled him.

"I'm headed to five myself." The corner of his mouth lifted in a smirk. "So I don't need another button."

Right. Idiot. Why hadn't she realized the obvious? Because her brain was still somewhat short-circuited from the brush of his fingers against hers? And here she'd thought *he'd* been flummoxed.

"But thanks for looking out for me," he added, still with that sexy half grin.

"Hey, it's what I do," she said, thinking of times she'd helped her siblings and the too-frequent occasions she'd felt compelled to "mother" Brad, which had led to their breakup. A woman couldn't feel passion for someone who aroused mostly her maternal instincts.

Her current companion didn't look as if he needed mothering, though. Quite the contrary. He looked like the type cautious mothers warned their daughters about.

"*This* is what you do?" he asked. "Look out for people in elevators?"

She smiled at his gently teasing tone. "I'm underappreciated, but, yes, I'm Sheryl, patron saint of elevators and caffeine addicts. And since you gave me such good advice down in the lobby and kept me from getting stuck in a faulty elevator, I'll put in a good word for you with The Guy Upstairs."

He chuckled. "I should introduce myself formally, then, so you get the name right when you make the recommendation." He stuck out his left hand. No wedding ring. "Nathan Zachary Hall, which I know sounds horribly like a dormitory."

Sheryl's smile froze. The elevator stopped and the doors parted, but it took great effort to force her feet forward, onto a busy fifth floor alongside...Nathan?

"*You're* Nathan Hall?" Even the dimmest bulb would be able to deduce he was, since he'd just said so, but he bore no resemblance to any of her beady-eyed, furry green imaginings.

"That's me." His once teasing tone was now puzzled.

He—a guy with a sense of humor who could wear jeans like that—was her nemesis?

As Meka would say, yikes.

2

NATHAN FELT A LITTLE SILLY standing there in front of so many desks and cubicles where his co-workers could witness this odd exchange. But the cacophony of buzzing phones, chirping computers and occasional cursing of the frustrated reporter assured him that people had better things to do than watch him. Besides, even if they'd all been staring, Nathan found he couldn't do much more than stand and wait for the brunette with the striking green eyes to say something.

Hoping to prompt a response, he picked up where the conversation had inexplicably derailed. "*I'm* Nathan Hall," he reiterated, in case there was any lingering confusion on that point. "And you are?"

"Sheryl." She addressed the floor more than him. But her seeming shyness was incongruous with the woman who had been joking with him just moments ago.

A smile touched his lips. "Right, Sheryl, the patron saint of elevators."

She looked up then, and if eyes were the window to the soul, then Sheryl had pulled the drapes tightly down over her exotic, slightly tilted cat's eyes. He'd had some experience reading people, but he couldn't get a handle on her current thoughts or mood. Nervous? Maybe even a little guilty about something? But resolved, too, a woman who knew what she had to do even if she didn't particularly want to do it.

"Sheryl Dayton," she elaborated. "I, um, Brad Hammond sent me."

Nathan's stomach turned over. Good Lord. Twice in his career, when he'd been working on investigative pieces, he'd been offered hush money from different corporations without soul or scruples, and a lower-level Mafia member had once made the much less tempting offer of breaking Nathan's legs if he pursued a story. Surely Hammond hadn't sent Nathan a *woman?*

She squared her shoulders and took a deep breath, her chest rising and falling under her sweater in a way he wished he hadn't noticed. "I'm in charge of Hammond's public relations depart—"

"You're HGS's PR man?" She couldn't be further from a man, but for once Nathan didn't care about semantics.

Well, he'd certainly been a pompous idiot to think even for a second that she might be a...what? Hooker? As though *anything* about the straight, sophisticated cut of her hair, her china-delicate skin, or the classy clothes that clung just softly enough to her slim curves to be sexy, suggested an illicit lifestyle. Apparently, his years of reporting about the worst in people were taking their toll on his judgment.

The only reason he could possibly have had for instantly linking Sheryl with sex was the attraction he felt to her. His immediate and appreciative masculine response to her physical appearance had only been heightened by their teasing in the elevator, the single potent touch they'd shared, and the way her interested gaze had brushed over his skin. He firmly ignored that attraction now to follow what she was saying.

"...to discuss those columns you've been writing." Her expression, if not actually frosty, was cool, her tone all business.

He matched her demeanor, folding his arms across his chest. "I have no intention of retracting a single word I've written so far, and if any new information surfaces, you can be sure there will be more columns. I'm sorry you wasted a trip across town."

"Maybe if we could just go in your office and talk—"

"If you wanted to talk, you should have made an appointment," he interrupted, pointing out the polite, professional course of action. "I'm a busy man, and I'm afraid I have a schedule to keep."

He wasn't born yesterday, and he had no intentions of letting her ambush him, as so clearly had been her plan. Manipulative. She'd arrived, scheming to surprise him, catching him off guard, but he'd turned the tables on her before she'd even stepped off the elevator. Nice irony, even if it had been unintentional.

Besides, though he did technically have his own office, the tiny room was actually smaller than some cubicles he'd seen. He wasn't prepared to be alone in that tight space with Sheryl and the light, teasing tang of her perfume.

Determined to sound in control of the situation, he invited casually, "Feel free to call the receptionist, though, and see if there's a way to squeeze you in next week. Maybe we'll talk then. Have a nice day, Ms. Dayton."

Her eyes sparked green flame, but she'd yet to form a reply when he spun on his heel and walked off, cheerfully whistling a Christmas carol.

"So we'll try again," Brad said from behind the me-
tallic-looking monstrosity that was his desk. Meka had
almost had a stroke when he'd insisted on it, and
Sheryl personally thought that it looked like a reject
from the *Star Trek* prop room. But Brad seemed to feel
the sci-fi aura of the piece was in keeping with running
a company known for technological successes in the
new millennium.

"Try again?" Sheryl banged a fist on the desk, too
angry to care that she'd probably just broken a couple
of fingers. "May I remind you, I was against this the
first time. The man wouldn't even let me into his office,
and you want me to go back for more abuse?"

Her ego was still smarting from the earlier encoun-
ter. All the polished words she'd practiced in the car on
her way to the *Sojourner* building had been reduced to
her gaping outside an elevator when she came face-to-
face with the man. But, considering the face in question, who could blame her?

Not a fan of conflict, Brad fidgeted, his pale blue eyes
nervous. Now that she thought about it, even though
his looks were classically handsome, his coloring, from
his eyes to his platinum-blond hair, was all pale, not at
all warm and vibrant like—

She snapped the thought in half like a dry twig.

"Uh...Sheryl, sweetie, did you just growl?"

She winced, but blasting Brad for the unprofessional
endearment probably wasn't the best way to reassure
him she wasn't rabid. "Course not. Cleared my
throat." She did so now for emphasis. *Ahem, ahem, hack,
hack, hack. See? Sick, not psychotic.* "I may be coming
down with a cold or something."

"I could have Iris order you some chicken soup from
the deli for lunch," he volunteered, concern in his gaze.

With a shake of her head, Sheryl reflected that he really *was* a nice guy. "That's all right." Sensing an opportunity to escape before he ordered her into a second round with Nathan Hall, she stood. "I have some cough drops in my desk and—"

"I've got some right here." He pulled open the slanted top drawer of his hybrid architecture/science-fair project and passed her a handful of honey-eucalyptus drops. "You just help yourself, and we can finish discussing this."

It had been worth a try.

She sat with a thud. "Brad, you hired me because you said you needed me, needed the advice that I and others have to give you. You're a brilliant man, but everyone has their strengths and weaknesses, and you pay us to balance yours out. So, please consider my advice when I tell you—"

"I considered your advice yesterday, Sheryl, when we had this same conversation. But we need this man to be our friend."

"It doesn't work that way! He doesn't want to befriend us, and we don't 'need' him, he's just one guy. Let's focus on—"

"Just one guy! I can't believe my public relations person just blew off a journalist with a direct pipeline to the public's opinion. You're a helluva lot smarter than that, so why are you being so stubborn about this, Sheryl?"

Because about two minutes before he introduced himself and subsequently kicked me out of the office, I was thinking I wouldn't kick him out of bed?

Hardly a professional answer, and she had other objections, too, dammit, she just couldn't remember them all right now. The entire time she and Brad were dating, she'd wished he'd develop a bit more of a backbone. She was proud of him for doing so, but did he have to pick now to do it?

"Well. You are the boss," she finally conceded.

"I'm so glad somebody remembered," he said. "I think you all see me as a little boy playing executive, but this is my company, you know?"

"I know." She glanced down guiltily, remembering the virtual shack in which he'd started his business four years ago and how far he'd already come—how far he'd taken all of them—with his ideas. There had been a time when the tiny company was so informal, it had been more like a club, and while that briefly had been fun, an enjoyable work atmosphere, she was proud of all they'd done to make Hammond Gaming Software the "real" business it was now.

Though she wasn't yet being paid a third of the salary Brad had said he envisioned for her future, no one else would have hired a woman with her limited experience for a position at this level. With a few notable exceptions, most of Brad's employees were young, well-trained, eager executives who wouldn't be able to find their current levels of autonomy elsewhere. The trade-off was that Brad had only recently begun to afford anything close to equitable salaries—luckily, the majority of his young execs didn't have families to support.

But he'd offered them a piece of his vision, combining their collective business acumen with his software smarts and wide-eyed optimism. He wanted to give them all a shot at the big time, and until a fantasy writer from Colorado with an obscure Web site had filed a lawsuit, Brad's master plan had seemed to be running smoothly.

She sighed. "What do you want me to do? Just say the word."

"Make sure Nathan comes to our office Christmas party a week from tomorrow," he insisted, sitting back in his ergonomic chair. "I want him to get to know us, see we're good people."

If only life were that simple. "I can ask him, but I can't guarantee he'll attend."

"Unless he already has plans he can't or won't get out of, why wouldn't he? He writes for a paper, and I'm essentially offering him an opportunity to spend time with HGS personnel and investigate. Why turn that down?"

And if one of their personnel inadvertently said something that got taken out of context on the front page? "Will you at least run the idea by Mark for his legal opinion and..." She trailed off since Brad was already shaking his head.

"I respect your opinion, Sheryl, you know that, and Mark's, too, but I've made up my mind on this."

"All right." If she wasn't going to win this, she might as well lose gracefully. "I'll go see Nathan again."

"Make an appointment this time," Brad advised, blue eyes twinkling. "You'll probably get further."

Her cheeks flooded with stinging warmth, and she felt compelled to defend herself. "I had a strategy—"

"We don't want to look like calculating people with a strategy. We want to look like exactly what we are— open and honest with nothing to hide. Once he realizes that, Nathan Hall is bound to see things from our point of view."

She recalled Nathan's vehemence when he'd informed her he wouldn't retract a word and would continue to write about Hammond for the foreseeable future. See things from their point of view? Well, Christmas was the season of miracles, so she supposed she'd just have to make one.

SHERYL PAUSED in her conversation to Meka just long enough to sip the criminally overpriced movie-concession cola she'd bought. She would've ordered popcorn, too, but that would probably require a co-signed loan. Above, the theater lights were still lit, and various pre-movie advertisements flashed across the screen. Tyler was meeting them here, and he still had a few minutes before showtime.

Replacing her cup in its plastic holder, she leaned back in her padded chair, concluding her rundown of today's meeting with Brad and his newest plan of action for handling Nathan Hall. "I know I've said dozens of times that if Brad is going to run his own company, he needs to be more assertive—"

"But you didn't really mean more assertive with you." Meka's smile was knowing.

"Exactly. So am I a big hypocrite?"

"Not so much hypocritical as frustrated by the whole situation," her friend said, absolving her. "But I have just the thing to take your mind off the so-called Boyfriend of Christmas Past."

"What's that?"

"The Boyfriend of Christmas Present."

"What?" There was no present boyfriend, and Sheryl currently preferred it that way.

"You've known me a few years," Meka said. "Have you ever seen me as happy as I am with Ty?"

"No." The two lovebirds were cute together, even if their evident love for each other was occasionally nauseating. "But that has nothing to do with me."

"You're unhappy. You've been so stressed—"

"Brad is paying lawyers money he should be spending on other things." Darting a quick glance around the theater, she lowered her voice. "Do you realize what could happen to us if, heaven forbid, the case actually goes to court and we lose? Of course I've been stressed!"

"But even before that Mathers woman claimed Hammond stole her story, you seemed unhappy. I want to see you happy, Sheryl, and I think the right guy would help with that."

"Maybe, but the right guy is going to have to wait until a better time." And Sheryl didn't just mean the work stuff.

Other people, such as her family, her co-workers and roommates, had often taken center stage in her life. Boyfriends who, though not all as emotionally draining as Brad had been, cut into what little time she might have had for herself.

"I figured you'd say that," Meka said. "Which is why I've decided not to take no for an answer."

Sheryl laughed. "What, you've decided to find me the right guy against my will?" When her roommate bit her lower lip and said nothing, Sheryl scowled. "What aren't you telling me?"

Not making eye contact, Meka sipped her own five-dollar soda and stalled.

Warning, warning. Red alert. "Tameka!"

"Look, it's nothing big, just that Ty isn't coming straight from work, he's coming from a squash match with a co-worker.... And he's bringing the co-worker with him."

"You set me up on a blind date? You set me up on a blind date *and didn't tell me!*" Ouch, Sheryl thought, rubbing one hand against her ear. When had she turned into such a shrill soprano?

"Don't think of it as a date so much as four people who all wanted to see this movie. Coincidentally at the same time and location."

"I can't believe this. I should leave right now on sheer principle."

"With Ty and Jonathan already on their way? Besides, I know how much you like the lead actor. You're not going anywhere after you've already bought your ticket."

Sheryl drummed her fingers on the purple plastic armrest between her and her supposed best friend. "I suppose you or Tyler told the guy—what's his name?"

"Jonathan Spencer. He's an accountant at the firm with Ty."

"So you guys have briefed Jonathan on me?"

"Absolutely."

"Yet you didn't bother to mention any of this to your own roommate," Sheryl grumbled.

"If it makes you less mad at me, we made you sound terrific. *I* wanted to date you by the time we finished describing you."

Sheryl laughed grudgingly. "As long as neither of you described me as having a 'good personality.'"

"Never!" Meka grinned, obviously knowing she was safely away from the edge of the thin ice. "We told him the truth, that you're sarcastic and opinionated on a good day, and downright unbearable if you haven't had enough coffee."

Grabbing her purse, Sheryl rummaged for something small to throw at her friend. Although bigger would work, too.

"Relax," Meka said, "we told him you had great legs

and an impressive job. Men secretly yearn for powerful women. And we've still got time before the guys get here for me to fill you in on Jonathan's vital statistics."

"Well, okay then. But you're never going to blind-side me like this again, right?"

"I won't need to, now that you know The Plan."

"The Plan?" Oh, boy. "You don't just mean Jonathan, do you?"

"Only if Jonathan miraculously turns out to be The One. But it'll probably take more than one guy—"

"Meka! How many men do you and Tyler have lined up and waiting in the wings? You can't just trot them all out and ask me to pick one."

"Clearly you don't watch reality TV. The networks seem to think that's exactly how people pair up." Her friend made a disdainful noise. "Look, I know love happens in its own time, but to fall in love with a guy, you gotta actually spend some time with a few."

Since Sheryl wasn't convinced she wanted to fall in love, she said nothing.

Meka wisely switched tactics. "Okay, even if you don't find your Ty, you'll have a selection of potential escorts for holiday parties and stuff like that. Besides, wouldn't it be fun to double date occasionally? Between the time I spend with Ty and your working late, I hardly see you anymore. I know you want your own place, but I don't want us to completely drift apart!"

Sighing, Sheryl conceded defeat. "Oh, all right, so I'll agree to a few harmless double dates." Put like that, it didn't seem she had anything to get riled up about.

Besides, maybe there'd be some chemistry between her and one of these bachelors, a spark that would prove she could have a powerful reaction to someone *besides* Nathan Hall.

3

WHY DIDN'T SHE HAVE one of those headsets like the one Denise had, Sheryl wondered on Friday. It had to beat scrunching the phone between your shoulder and ear while you tried to get some work done. By eleven, Sheryl felt as if she'd already talked to a hundred people.

Of course, she'd had three calls in the past hour from Mom alone. First, she wanted to remind Sheryl about the family dinner the weekend before Christmas in addition to the actual gathering on Christmas Day, then she called back to ask if Sheryl had made any headway in her shopping, or if her mother should pick up gifts for the kids in the family and put Sheryl's name on the tags. Feeling somewhat diminished by the suggestion she couldn't be trusted to shop for her nieces and nephew, Sheryl had of course lied and said her holiday shopping was well under control.

Then Mom called one final time because she'd forgotten to ask what Sheryl herself wanted for Christmas. So, *ha*, obviously Sheryl wasn't the only one not quite finished with shopping. Not quite finished, hadn't bought so much as the first present or the paper to wrap it in—all depended on how you looked at it.

Too bad Mom knew her direct extension, or Sheryl could instruct Denise to run interference at the main switchboard and claim Sheryl had left for the day.

Luckily, most of the other calls had been pleasant and productive. Two years ago, with Brad's whole-hearted approval and their accountant's assurance of tax write-offs, Sheryl had organized a community Christmas festival that helped to raise money for area families in need. Other sponsors had joined in with HGS, and the event had become an annual tradition. School counselors had been calling all morning with this year's updated list of needy families.

So far, it looked as though the turnout for the HGS Holiday Festival on the nineteenth would be even bigger than it had been the past two years, which meant more people would be assisted. It felt great to be Santa Claus, and the festival couldn't have come at a better time, publicity-wise. Sheryl and her assistant, Grace, had already lined up local performers and food vendors, and a volunteer committee of HGS employees was devising different contests for kids of varying ages. Brad himself would act as the final judge for all the competitions.

Pleased with her accomplishments, Sheryl consulted her to-do list of everything she wanted to achieve before lunch, and her mood took a sharp bah-humbug turn. *Call Nathan Hall's office and arrange appointment.* She should do that immediately to give him the most advance notice of the Christmas party and increase his chances of being able to attend. Squirming in her seat, she admitted to herself that she *should* have called yesterday. But she'd just been so busy...

Her fingers reached for the phone with all the enthusiasm she usually reserved for doctors' appointments that involved stirrups.

But the receptionist who answered was a cheerful woman who easily accommodated Sheryl with a meeting first thing Tuesday morning, so maybe Nathan's schedule wasn't quite as jam-packed as he'd insinuated. Which confirmed her suspicion that his refusal to talk with her had been a power move—very annoying, even if she had shown up unannounced for the same reason.

No sooner had Sheryl disconnected than the persistent red light for line one flashed again, a mere second before the distinct buzz that indicated a call was coming through. *If it's Mom again, I'm asking Brad to authorize a new extension for me.* "Sheryl Dayton."

"Ah, um, Sheryl, I hope you don't mind, but Tameka gave me your personal ex—oh, this is Jonathan Spencer. We, ah, met last night."

"I remember," she assured him.

They'd sat next to each other through the two-hour movie, then joined Tyler and Meka for a late snack at a local diner. Jonathan had seemed nice enough, though to be honest, *not* particularly memorable, which, judging from his nervous tone, he realized. But she was sure there was more to the man than she'd glimpsed last night. He was probably a wonderful guy just waiting to be found by the right lucky woman.

He cleared his throat. "I don't usually call women this soon after first meeting them—didn't want you to think I was desperate or, ah, you know, a stalker—but this morning a client gave me two tickets to *The Nutcracker* tomorrow night. I thought if you're not already busy, you might like to go with me?"

Well, since Meka wasn't available for that girls' night out this weekend, Sheryl didn't really have plans. Besides, she needed to work on her holiday spirit this year, and she hadn't seen the ballet since she was a little girl. Maybe *Nutcracker* was just what she needed.

"That sounds great Jonathan, thanks for thinking of me. What time's the show?"

He answered promptly, as though afraid she'd change her mind if he didn't, and volunteered to pick her up. "Would you like to have dinner beforehand?"

Sheryl did a quick mental analysis. He'd been awfully quiet last night. Maybe just because he was too polite to talk during movies, and Meka and Ty had monopolized conversation afterwards. Still, if Jonathan were as silent Saturday evening, it could make for a long dinner.

"I have a ton of shopping that I'll be doing tomorrow," she demurred, "and it may run into the early evening. Why don't we just go to the show and maybe coffee afterwards?"

A good compromise, she thought. And in case of a true dating emergency, like he belched to the melody of *Dance of the Sugar Plum Fairy* or excused himself during intermission to call his wife, she'd claim unforeseen exhaustion and ask to go straight home. Of course, she seriously doubted he'd do either of those things, but a smart single gal didn't overlook a possible escape route on a first date.

THE DOORBELL RANG at seven sharp. Whatever else could be said about Jonathan Spencer, he was punctual. Sheryl opened the door with a welcoming smile.

"You look nice," Jonathan said immediately, as though he'd rehearsed his greeting.

Almost as an afterthought, he ran a quick glance down the forest-green, ankle-length velvet sheath she wore under a matching mock duster of green-and-black velvet. The long jacket was edged in black satin at the cuffs and lapels. She'd be plenty warm, the outfit just wasn't very water-resistant. Those weathermen who'd promised a clear, starry night with a record-breaking lack of precipitation had better have known what they were talking about.

"You, too," she said, taking in his blue suit and pin-stripe tie.

Jonathan *was* good-looking, she realized absently. Average height, he had coloring reminiscent of the beach—thick sandy hair and oceanic aquamarine eyes. So why was she only just now noticing he was attractive and even then in a detached, he'd-make-a-good-date-for-my-sister, kind of way? Here stood a reasonably handsome man with a good job, acceptable table manners and cultured enough not to feel like a sissy attending the ballet. Frankly, after a few of the bad dates she and Meka had discussed in their collective pasts, the table manners alone put him ahead of some of the men out there. But there was no sense of anticipation or attraction, no flutter of first-date nerves.

Nonetheless, she smiled brightly and grabbed her black handbag off of a hook near the front door. "Where's the performance? I didn't think to ask when you called yesterday. The Paramount? Mercer Arts Center?"

"Actually, it's at a place I'm not familiar with, but I got the map off the Web." He retrieved two tickets from his jacket pocket, studying one quizzically. She just made out the word *Nutcracker* before he folded the tickets back into his pocket. "The Backstage Pass?"

Sheryl could feel her eyebrows zoom up and disappear beneath her bangs. "The Backstage Pass, really?"

How many theaters in Seattle could there be by that

name? She'd been there twice, once as a requirement for a college elective, and once in the pre-Ty days when Meka had been dating a would-be actor. Tameka would roll on the floor laughing when Sheryl told her she'd gone back.

The Backstage Pass specialized in bizarre, experimental performances, and while Sheryl wasn't a regular theater buff, she also wasn't a total neophyte to the Seattle arts scene. She'd seen a couple of truly wonderful alternative pieces in this city, but not at the Backstage Pass. The play she'd seen in college—billed as a "romance" —consisted of a man and woman standing on stage for a solid hour quoting verses from obscure poems on love while playing Ping-Pong. In the nude.

The program explained that the nudity represented men's and women's desire for true intimacy and no barriers, while the indoor tennis table was a metaphor for the games that people play anyway, preventing that very intimacy. Sheryl got all that, but she figured that if you had to explain the symbolism, it probably wasn't working very well. Besides, though there was nothing at all vulgar about the tedious, vaguely pretentious one-act, some people just weren't meant to be naked in front of an audience. Particularly if they were going to dive energetically to the left to volley an opponent's serve.

The second time she'd gone—to support Tameka and watch the boyfriend who'd generously and inaccurately called himself an actor—the play hadn't even aspired to something as lofty as symbolism. It had been simple shock theater, designed to offend audiences, and, if failing to raise that level of emotion, then at least gross them out.

What was a place like that doing with a traditional holiday ballet like *Nutcracker?*

"Anything wrong?" Jonathan asked, snapping her back to the present.

"Um..." He already seemed nervous about tonight; she didn't want to say anything that might be construed as a complaint this early in the evening.

Maybe it won't be so bad.

For all she knew, the place was under new management. The show's title was at least the same, a good sign. If they were doing some sort of revisionist adaptation, didn't they normally alter the name? *The Wiz*, for example, had been a jazzed-up version of *The Wizard of Oz*. If Jonathan had said the show was called *Crackin' The Nut*, then she'd have reason to worry.

She kicked her smile up another notch, hoping she didn't look like some phony, cheerful early-morning news anchor. "Nope, everything is just fine."

Of course, two hours later, she wished that instead of being polite she'd advised Jonathan that they run, not walk, in the opposite direction of the theater to seek out other entertainment. Because "entertaining" certainly didn't describe the evening she was being subjected to.

When they'd arrived, Sheryl had noticed that she and Jonathan seemed overdressed compared to most of the other patrons. But it wasn't until they reached the ushers at the front of the auditorium that she noticed the billboard: Nutcracker! and then in much smaller print underneath, "A dark, urbanized retelling of the original tale." Oh, good, just what Christmas needed—dark urbanization.

As Jonathan followed her gaze, he began to look nervous—even more so than before—and immediately retrieved the tickets from his pocket, squinting at the small print. "I had no idea," he stammered. "A client gave... I saw the first word and just assumed..."

"It's all right," she told him, feeling guilty now for not having shared her misgivings about the Backstage. "Maybe it'll be..." She hadn't been able to think of a word, but it hadn't mattered because then it was their turn to hand over their tickets and find their seats.

Now, it was intermission, and Sheryl didn't know how much more she could take. The play had begun with slightly altered characters Claire and Franz giving disturbed soliloquies on their relationships with their parents. Due to a dysfunctional home life, they joined a gang led by an underworld figure known as the Rat King. Then followed several violent, badly choreographed street-fight/dance numbers accompanied by an overpowering electric guitar. The program promised that in the next half of the show, the traditional dance of sweets was being replaced by Claire hallucinating that different narcotics had come to life.

As soon as the lights went up in the auditorium, Sheryl bolted for the main lobby, a dazed Jonathan following behind. Was there a polite way to ask him if they could just cut their losses and leave? He'd been the one to invite her, and if she suggested going now, she might make him feel worse. *Please, get us out of here*, she willed him, feeling the bright red walls around them closing in on her.

He shoved his hands in his trouser pockets. "Um, Sheryl, I was wondering if—"

"Yes?" she prompted, trying not to sound too eager while fighting the urge to shout, "Race you to the car!"

"—you'd like a drink?"

Damn. So close. "Yes, please. A drink sounds..." *Necessary.* "Refreshing."

He told her he'd see if they served any white wines and shuffled off through the crowd of theater-goers, some of whom looked appalled, some of whom were raving about the "bold, new vision," and some of whom were laughing hysterically and cracking jokes about how the play should end. Finding a few of the alternate endings humorous, Sheryl stood near the top of a stairwell and shamelessly eavesdropped, occasionally scooting over to make room for someone to get by, but not really paying attention to her surroundings until she experienced a little jolt. It felt like a mild, but not unpleasant, electric shock.

Glancing around to make sure there were no exposed wires anywhere near her, she caught the dark-roast gaze of Nathan Hall. The fact that his mere presence had given her a warm tingle was more disturbing than the on-stage spectacle.

Now what? She didn't particularly want to speak to him, but since he was standing only yards away and they were staring into each other's eyes... She blinked purposefully.

Nathan walked around the people surrounding him and strode toward her. Not as dressed up as she in her velvet or Jonathan in his suit, Nathan looked great in a long-sleeved graphite shirt and black pants that were mercifully baggier than the jeans she'd last seen him in.

Of course, instead of evaluating his sartorial choices, she should have been working on an opening line, because when he stopped directly in front of her, what she unthinkingly blurted was, "What are *you* doing here?"

His eyes narrowed as he scowled, and she immediately regretted her words. She shouldn't further antagonize the very columnist Brad aspired to win over.

Before Nathan could retort to her rudeness, she hastily amended, "I didn't mean that personally, it was more a what-would-any-right-thinking-person-be-doing-here kind of question."

Oh, hell, had she just insinuated he wasn't right-thinking? Worse, what if he actually liked this type of theater? How had she landed a job in public relations, anyway, if her communication skills were this bad?

But Nathan smiled at her comment, though unintentionally by the looks of it. His quick, genuine grin gave way to a slightly startled expression, then a carefully neutral mask. "You aren't enjoying the ballet?"

She shuddered. "It's awful."

"I know. Kaylee's gonna owe me big time for this."

"Kaylee?" Maybe he had a sister, she thought hopefully. Annoyed for caring, she mollified herself with the rationalization that she had kind of flirted with him the other day and she would feel bad about flirting with another woman's boyfriend.

"My date," he said. "She writes for the Arts section and was sent to cover this nightmare. You can read all about it in the *Sojourner*."

"As it happens, I don't spend my money on that publication." Too late, she bit her tongue, wondering what had happened to her resolve not to antagonize.

But he made the switch to antagonism without missing a beat. "I understand I have an appointment with you next week. I appreciate your going through conventional channels, but if you're coming to grovel, I should tell you now your time would be better off picking out a Christmas tree or something. I'm not backing off your crooked employer."

"Crooked! Brad Hammond is a great man. Not just

as a business visionary and software genius, but a legitimately *nice* person."

"If your definition of *nice* involves stealing," Nathan retorted. "Are you telling me you honestly believe the similarities between Brad Hammond's game and Kendra Mathers's story—a story that first appeared on her site long before the public had any information on *Xandria Quest*—can be chalked up to coincidence?"

Not about to comment on the case, she focused only on his first sentence. "My definition of *nice* sure as hell doesn't involve making snap judgments about people I don't know, but am more than happy to vilify in order to sell a few papers!"

"I do *not* make snap judg—" But Nathan cut himself off. She wondered if it was because he had in fact recently leapt to a conclusion about someone, or simply because he'd noticed people were beginning to stare.

Jonathan appeared at the edge of the group of onlookers, and muttering pardon me to several of them, reached Sheryl's side. "Your wine. I hope white Zinfandel is all right?"

"Sure, thanks," she murmured, annoyed with the effort it took to pull her gaze away from Nathan's face and turn to her date. "Jonathan Spencer, Nathan Hall."

"Oh, the reporter?" Jonathan asked brightly. "You did a great series on industrial effects on the waterfront! How you took such dry statistics and presented both the pros and cons of commercialization..."

NATHAN NODDED and managed a gracious response to Jonathan's words, but it was difficult to concentrate on anything other than Sheryl Dayton. She riled him, no escaping that, but it helped to know he had a mutual effect on her. He doubted that a woman who made her living in PR usually lost her temper.

How devoted to her job was she, he wondered? Would she defend her company even if she knew it was in the wrong simply because she was paid to? Nathan understood the necessity of a paycheck, but in his journalism career, he'd seen too many people sell out their scruples.

Not that he should care so much about Sheryl Dayton, but it bothered him to know he might be attracted to a woman with shady ethics. And he *was* attracted to her. Wrapped as she was in that slinky fall of soft fabric, which hugged her body and made her eyes glow, how could he not be?

To his right, the crowd parted like a sea before Moses, and a statuesque redhead made her way up the stairs, drawing admiring male stares as she passed. Nathan was used to the Kaylee Phenomenon, but he couldn't remember his beautiful co-worker ever delivering the kick to his libido that Sheryl Dayton did.

Kaylee stopped at his side with a sigh. "I'm back from the powder room. I suppose we have to watch Act Two now?"

"Only if you want your column to be accurate and well-informed," he kidded his co-worker.

She wrinkled her nose. "I'm pretty sure I could just turn in the words *save your money* and cover it. Oh, aren't you going to introduce me to your friends?"

Nathan did so, watching Sheryl's face as she met Kaylee. Most women looked intimidated or envious meeting the supermodel-caliber beauty for the first time, but Sheryl simply grinned and remarked on how awful the show was.

"Well," Kaylee said, "as long as we still have a minute, I should probably excuse myself to call my—"

"You'd better hurry," Nathan interjected. "I'm not watching this thing by myself."

She nodded and stepped outside for a better cell connection. Moments later, the lights blinked to signal the second half, and Sheryl and her date disappeared inside the auditorium. Standing in the lobby, Nathan watched them go, wondering whether he'd interrupted his co-worker specifically so she wouldn't have a chance to say she was calling her husband, who'd had to work tonight.

Had Nathan wanted Sheryl to think he was on a date just because she had been? Of course, Sheryl wouldn't know how ironic the idea of his dating Kaylee was. Not only was his friend and co-worker very happily married, she was the person who routinely insisted Nathan should date more.

He changed the subject whenever Kaylee brought it up, but she'd made it clear that she thought Nathan distrusted women because of his mom walking out when he was young. Apparently, Kaylee had been exposed to too much Freud one semester in college. The problems Nathan had in relationships had *nothing* to do with the mother he barely thought about and everything to do with individual circumstance. Sheryl Dayton was a perfect example.

Yes, he was drawn to Sheryl, he was man enough to admit that. But the inconvenient desire he'd felt both times he'd been around her wouldn't blur his principles. Her employer had boasted his aggressive company goals in numerous interviews, and if Nathan learned of concrete proof that the man's ambitions had led him to take advantage of a struggling writer without the same corporate legal resources, all of Seattle would read about it.

Sheryl wouldn't like it—wouldn't like *him*—but that was just too bad. Nathan's dad, a dedicated police officer, had spent hours lecturing him on integrity, and Nathan was determined to live up to his late father's ideals. The very ideals that had eventually broken up his parents' marriage.

Nathan would simply put Sheryl and his curiosity about which was softer, the velvety concoction she wore or her skin, out of his mind.

Although, he'd feel better about the sensible, uncompromising resolution if he weren't already thinking about seeing her Tuesday.

4

REMINDING HIMSELF that he'd dealt with dignitaries, celebrities and the mob, for heaven's sake, Nathan reached over his cluttered desktop and hit the intercom button on his phone. "Thanks for the heads-up," he told the receptionist, who'd buzzed him to say Sheryl was coming his way.

He was *not* nervous about this meeting. In all actuality, his slightly energized feeling was probably anticipation and not nerves at all. Then again, being this excited about seeing her again didn't seem like a good idea, either.

Nathan leaned back in his cheap, creaky chair—he must have unknowingly maligned the office supply manager to be assigned furniture so uniquely unsuited to sitting—recalling too late that the balance was slightly off and that the chair tilted back too far. He was scrambling to an upright position when Sheryl appeared in the open doorway. "Knock knock," she said in a wry tone.

Terrific. Not exactly the all-knowing, indomitable image he'd wanted to start off with, but he figured they were even now for her last visit to the office. He'd certainly thrown her for a loop when he'd caught her off guard with his identity.

He cleared his throat and moved to straighten his tie before recalling he didn't bother with ties at work. He had when he'd first started out, but soon realized his editors didn't care about his dress code as much as documented sources and word count.

"Good morning, Ms. Dayton. Please, have a seat."

Eyebrows raised over green eyes glinting with mirth, she considered the chair opposite him, a replica of the piece of unbalanced furniture he occupied. "Are we sure that's a good idea?" She glanced around the cubby-sized office, filled to capacity by a desk, two chairs and a wastebasket with a miniature basketball hoop suspended over the top. "Although, I suppose there isn't much standing room in here, is there?"

"The accommodations not up to your standards?" He tried to imagine her surroundings at HGS.

She surprised him with a bright laugh. "Are you kidding? This is *palatial* compared to the last building we were in. My office space was pretty much me working out of a box and sitting hunched over with a laptop literally in my lap. I guess that's how those things got their names. But Brad promised us we'd be moving on to greener pastures, and he kept his word."

At what cost? the insatiable reporter in Nathan wondered.

From what he'd read, Brad Hammond was driven to succeed. But driven enough to convince himself that "borrowing" a few ideas from an obscure writer in Colorado couldn't hurt anything?

Sheryl's eyes narrowed as though she knew exactly what he was thinking, but he wasn't going to apologize for doing his job. *Then is it fair to hold Sheryl's job against her?* a nagging little voice asked.

That was different, he assured himself as she settled into the proffered chair. He understood Sheryl's professional position required her to try to make HGS look good, but if she earned her salary by knowingly defending a thief...

"What was it that you wanted to talk to me about, exactly?" His tone was more abrupt than he'd intended, but she unsettled him in a way he hated. He preferred things as black-and-white as the newsprint of his column. These unpredictable, mixed reactions to Sheryl fell into a dangerously gray area.

She smoothed a theoretical wrinkle out of her charcoal-colored slacks, clearly using the gesture to stall for time. Nathan studied her while she silently selected the perfect public-relations words instead of shooting from the hip as she had at the theater when he'd last seen her. He found himself absurdly relieved that she wore a pantsuit now and not tantalizingly soft green velvet.

"I came to extend an invitation from Mr. Hammond," she said finally. "So far, you've only printed one side of the story and have chosen not to run any of our press releases—"

"The *Sojourner* is not in the habit of serving as a mouthpiece for any company, yours included. We write the news. But for what it's worth, I personally don't have anything to do with that decision. We have editors who make those calls."

Her cheeks darkened with color, and he watched with equal parts admiration and amusement as she fought back the irritation brightening her eyes. "You're right, of course. I didn't mean to imply that you personally were responsible. What I did want to do was let you know that Hammond Gaming Software's annual Christmas party is Friday night, and Br—Mr. Hammond wanted me to invite you."

"Really?"

Last time she'd been here, he'd had the impression she wanted to give him a tongue-lashing over his columns, not extend a Yuletide invitation. But he wasn't completely surprised by the friendly overture since he'd seen similar tactics in the past. Win the reporter over, try to get him in your pocket and generate press that was little more than unpaid advertising.

"You don't think that having me around would dampen the festive atmosphere?" Nathan asked.

"What I think about this doesn't matter," she retorted before biting her lip and cursing softly under her breath.

Nathan grinned. Obviously, she'd been against this invitation, and her candor was something he couldn't help appreciating. In the years since landing his first newspaper assignment, he'd run across too many disingenuous people who were appallingly comfortable with half truths and out-and-out lies.

"Are you always so blunt, Ms. Dayton? One would think it might hinder your ability to do your job."

She shook her head emphatically, sending her smooth dark ponytail swinging. "On the contrary, being a forthright person and working for a company I strongly believe in make it *easy* to do my job. Because I mean every word I say and stand by Hammond Gaming Software. I'm passionate about my work."

Firmly reining in his thoughts before they wandered to any other situations she might be passionate in, he said, "Loyalty's a nice quality." But he couldn't help wondering if hers was misplaced.

When she was sticking to her professional script, delivering sentences she'd obviously constructed before walking in the door, she called her boss Mr. Hammond. But a couple of times she'd slipped and referred to him as Brad. Not that this was unheard of, but there had been something in her expression... She hadn't exactly gone all gooey-eyed over the man or anything, but Nathan thought perhaps there was more than professional devotion at stake. Did she have a personal relationship with her employer?

Ignoring the irrational pang that arrowed through him at that possibility, he reasoned that the relationship couldn't amount to much if she'd been on a date with some other guy Saturday night. Oddly, the reminder of seeing her with another man did little to ease that inexplicable pang.

He steepled his fingers under his chin, admonishing himself to focus on something besides Sheryl Dayton's love life. "Can I ask you something, then, one forthright person to another? What does Brad Hammond hope to accomplish by inviting me to his shindig this weekend?"

This time, instead of brushing at nonexistent wrinkles, she toyed with the strap of her black leather handbag. Another obvious stall, but why? Because she didn't know how to answer, because she was censoring her answer? Was she trying to hide facts from him and finding it difficult with her frank nature?

"Mr. Hammond understands that your job is to report a story, and he wants to make sure that all the facts are available to you."

Cynicism left an acrid taste in Nathan's mouth. "Oh, so this is strictly for my benefit. He's trying to do me a favor, is that it? Kind man."

"Yes he is," she snapped, her eyes flashing. Once again, he had the sense that Sheryl wasn't speaking about a mere boss. She seemed at the very least protective of the man, and with a fierceness most people didn't show their employers. "But of course, this isn't a favor to you. He's hoping that once you get your facts straight—namely, that Hammond has been wrongly accused—you'll have enough journalistic integrity to share those facts with the rest of Seattle."

Any curiosity or attraction this woman generated in him now took a back seat to anger. "You're questioning *my* integrity?" He jerked a thumb at the handful of framed awards that hung in his otherwise undecorated office. "I've been applauded for honesty and diligence in the pursuit of the truth. You're the one who works for a man facing a lawsuit for theft."

Nathan winced inwardly at how pompous he sounded. Applauded for honesty and diligence in pursuit of the truth? Could he sound more full of himself?

Sheryl stood quickly, her shoulder bag banging against her thigh. "I appreciate your taking the time to see me today, Mr. Hall, but I sense that this meeting has not been productive. I'll just pass along your regrets and say that you'll be unable to attend Friday."

Her last sentence was said with such relief that Nathan couldn't help zeroing in on it. He shouldn't be surprised, she'd as much as admitted she didn't want him there when she'd issued the invitation. Was she worried that Brad Hammond might say or do something to incriminate himself?

Or—and this was a very likely possibility—did she just not like Nathan himself?

Whatever her reasons for hoping that he'd turn the invitation down, Nathan found he wanted to investigate further, to find out if there was more to this story than met the eye. *I have legitimate work-related reasons to go*, he assured himself, although he was too honest a man not to realize that part of his acceptance stemmed from a paradoxical desire to see her again.

Unsure whether the challenge in his tone was for her or himself, he answered, "On the contrary, Ms. Dayton." He grinned broadly. "I'll be there with bells on."

SEATTLE BOASTED some wonderful shopping, but not even a major sale on Kate Spade shoes would excite Sheryl right now.

Well...

Slowing her steps across the mall's tiled corridor, she reconsidered, absently registering the sound of an elementary-school bell choir playing for gathered listeners and the smell of oversized cinnamon rolls baking at a nearby kiosk. *Maybe* a shoe sale would brighten her afternoon or give her something to think about besides her earlier meeting with Nathan. But she doubted it.

You're supposed to be shopping for your family, she reminded herself. *Focus.*

After working late on the upcoming festival last night and arriving at the office today before sunrise to accomplish some things before her ill-fated meeting, she'd decided to treat herself to an extended lunch hour. Only she'd skipped the lunch part and advanced straight to Christmas shopping. Theoretically. So far she'd been wandering the mall aimlessly, halfheartedly nursing a latte, and hadn't set foot in a single store.

While she hadn't been thrilled by the animosity crackling in Nathan's office—a small space that had seemed to heighten everything from their differences of opinion to his rugged, striking features—she at least had been relieved by the assumption that he would refuse her invitation. He'd startled her with his last-minute acceptance.

I'll be there with bells on.

Did the man always have to have the last word? They'd gone on to exchange polite goodbyes, unlike his blatant dismissal of her after their first meeting. Still, he'd left her with the sense that he was always one up on her, and she felt the juvenile compulsion to even the score.

Since she'd been too stunned and blunt to mouth a professional half truth, such as she looked forward to seeing him there, couldn't she have made some sarcastic rejoinder to wipe the smirk off his face?

I'll be there with bells on.

Something like, "Actually, I believe the restaurant has a dress code."

Great. *Now* her sarcasm instincts kicked in.

When she'd walked into his office and seen him struggling with that dinosaur of an office chair, it should have lessened any attraction, made him seem comical. Instead, the moment had made her want to smile with him. She'd instantly flashed to the miniscule, tattered office space HGS had started out in.

Brad had been understandably adamant that they never scrimp on computer equipment, so they'd cut corners in other areas, making do with circumstances that were laughable in hindsight. When she'd first seen Nathan this morning, Sheryl had suddenly wanted to share anecdotes with him, watch him chuckle as he had that day in the elevator.

Not that it mattered how likable she found Nathan. He clearly held her company, if not Sheryl herself, in disdain. Why was he so sure of their guilt?

Admit it. The situation looks bad.

The timing of *Xandria Quest*'s release was the worst part. Coincidence was too big a stretch of the imagination when it came to the similarities between the detailed alternate dimensions, as well as actual character names, used in both the game and the story, so the question boiled down to, who had the idea first?

Kendra Mathers had been off in Colorado writing, hardly a likely suspect, such as a disgruntled HGS employee who might steal an idea and run with it. And her stories had been posted before the game ever landed on shelves, so it wasn't as though anyone could accuse her of lifting the idea, even subconsciously, after she saw it in stores.

If this case went to court, people would see her story as being "first." What their lawyer, Mark, would have to explain was how long *Xandria Quest* had been in development. It wasn't something that had cropped up at the last minute, regardless of when Kendra netpublished the first episode of her story.

Sheryl's stomach clenched as worry ate at her insides.

Shop. That was the answer. Clearance-sale therapy. Nothing felt quite as good as finding someone just the right gift *and* discovering it at an enviable discount.

Pitching her now-cold latte into a nearby garbage can, she decided to seek out items for her dad, brother and brother-in-law. They were the easiest, since they tended to want manly presents like power tools. She could shop in one place for all of them, without internal debate over color, size or necessary matching jewelry.

One electric drill, two jigsaw blades, three router bits and four metaphorical calling birds later, Sheryl reemerged in the main mall corridor, slowing near a bench to adjust the weight of her purchases and her shoulder bag. For daytime use, she packed a purse with an eye toward function, not daintiness. Unfortunately, it got heavy fast, especially when combined with power tools. Oh, okay, power tools *and* one gorgeous, half-off pair of boots she'd seen on her way into the department store and hadn't been able to resist.

Half off! She'd practically been *obligated* to purchase them.

But she had a plan to redeem her moment of weakness—the boots would be an excellent Christmas present for Meka, who luckily had great taste, the same foot size and was generous about sharing. Thinking of Meka, Sheryl wished she'd called her roommate and asked her to meet up for lunchtime shopping. Her friend had spent the past few nights at Tyler's place, and though Sheryl had enjoyed having the apartment to herself, she was dying to hear details about meeting the parents.

Ready to conquer a few more stores, Sheryl glanced up, looking for a mall directory to inspire her. Her gaze landed on a boutique window where modernized, too-thin, bald mannequins without facial features wore fabulous party dresses for the holiday season. Sheryl's feet had already taken a half-dozen steps in that direction before she rediscovered her willpower.

What was she thinking?

Of that little red number between the black sequined one and the green sweater dress.

The trendy boutique didn't seem anywhere in the same zip code as affordable. At least not for a gal with a ton of Christmas shopping left, as well as looming repairs on a car she'd *meant* to call a mechanic about before getting preoccupied with Nathan Hall issues.

Nathan. Would he bring a date to the Christmas party?

Remembering the stunner who'd been on his arm at the Backstage Pass, Sheryl took a few more involuntary steps toward the beckoning red dress with the slightly plunging V-neck and just-off-the-shoulder straps. Would *she* have a date for the party?

Jonathan Spencer was out of the question. Poor man. As she'd unlocked her apartment door Saturday night, he'd placed a hand on her arm, stopping her. She'd feared an awkward good-night kiss, but instead, he'd sighed and said, out of the blue, "I have a sister."

Before she could even decide whether or not she wanted to guess where that strange opener was leading, he followed up with, "And I know she hates it when guys say they'll call and then, you know, don't. So let's be honest. Tonight didn't, um, go all that well. Let's assume that we'll both go on to have nice lives and not, ah, hear from each other."

Then he'd practically bolted down the stairs, leaving Sheryl amused that he'd ended the date with a "Don't call me, I won't call you" disclaimer.

Anyway, Sheryl should probably go alone to the Christmas party, leave herself free to keep an eye on Brad and make sure no one said anything Nathan Hall might take the wrong way and pass on to the front page.

But just because she'd be going stag didn't mean she couldn't look good, her feet reasoned as they marched her inside the pricey boutique. Making one last ditch effort at mind over matter, she told herself the color of the dress was all wrong. With the natural highlights in her burnished brown hair, red would probably clash. *Why not try it on, then?* If it didn't suit her, she could put it back on its hanger with no regrets, affordability a moot point.

A coifed and styled saleswoman swooped in immediately, cooing, "That dress is *you*, dear."

Though Sheryl's gut instinct agreed, she had the feeling the woman would have said "It's you" even if Sheryl had been eyeing the fuzzy fuchsia minidress that looked as though it would shed like a pack of Persian cats.

Taking a delicate yet unshakable hold on Sheryl's elbow, the commission-motivated woman herded her toward the dressing rooms. She had Sheryl safely locked inside one within seconds.

Succumbing to the inevitable, Sheryl discarded her pantsuit and pulled on the dress…that appeared to be made for her. The fabric was sleek, but simple. Nothing fussy that might make her feel overdressed, just quality material and elegant lines.

The almost daring bodice folded gracefully into a gently flared skirt that was neither long enough to fall in the evening gown category, nor short enough to raise eyebrows at the Japanese restaurant hosting the party. Rather than clash with her hair, the red color gave her a dramatic aura. The fit was strangely perfect, too. Not tight, but *exact*.

At the risk of seeming immodest, she could honestly turn some heads Friday night. Men aside, she owed it to womankind to buy this dress. It was fate, serendipity, kismet—how often did a woman at the mall happen into The Perfect Dress when she hadn't even been looking for one?

She changed back into her own clothes before she could talk herself out of the extravagant purchase, and the saleswoman happily led her to the cash register. As

Sheryl completed the transaction, a chirping sound alerted her to her cell phone ringing inside the large purse.

That would be my conscience calling. "Sheryl Dayton speaking."

"It's Brad. Sorry I was in a meeting when you got back. How'd it go?"

Holding the phone with her shoulder, Sheryl put away the credit card the saleswoman had just handed back, surprised the little piece of plastic wasn't smoking. "It went the way you'd hoped. Didn't you get the message I left?"

"Well, yeah, but I wanted to speak directly to you. How'd it *go?*" he repeated with B-movie emphasis, as though he were asking in code for the secret formula she'd been sent to retrieve.

"He seemed offended by the invitation," she said, knowing it wouldn't be what Brad wanted to hear, "but he accepted it anyway. I think he's only coming to see if he can find anything else he can print about us."

"No problem. Because there isn't anything bad he can print about us, and he seems fair. Eventually, he may have to write something good about us."

"I hope so." And she did. Not just because it would be best for HGS, but because it would be nice to see Nathan on her side. Maybe if there wasn't opposition between them—

"I also called to see if there was anything else you needed to discuss with me today. I'll probably be gone when you get back this afternoon," Brad reminded her. "Wanted to leave early to make an evening appointment. My therapist, you know."

"I know," she echoed, wondering if now would be the time to fake a bad connection and hang up.

"You sure you won't go with me? Dr. Engvall says that it's very common to invite friends and family to participate, so he might understand the patient better. You're not only the last serious romantic relationship I had, but a colleague who could shed some light on my current work environ—"

"Sss...can't...I—sss. Brad, you still there? I think I've lost you," she said over his reply. Then she hit the button that disconnected them. If reason wouldn't work with the man, there was always cellular static.

Of course, she'd just paid money she didn't have in order to impress a man who appeared to date supermodels and would see Sheryl on Friday only because he intended to dig up dirt on the company responsible for paying her rent. Maybe Brad wasn't the only one who needed to chat with a therapist.

5

TAMEKA WHISTLED. "Girl, you look hot. You definitely made the right choice buying it for the party."

Sheryl turned from side to side, glancing down. She'd been half afraid that the dress's flattering qualities had somehow been a trick of strategic in-store lighting. "It does look pretty good, doesn't it?"

"Whatever you paid was worth it," Meka guaranteed from her position sprawled out across Sheryl's double bed. "I'd beg to borrow it, but with our differences in height, it would be awkward on me."

Sheryl reached for her very unglamorous flannel pajamas. "So enough about me and my shopping weaknesses, when do I get to hear all about the big meeting?"

"Oh. That."

Troubled by her friend's uncharacteristic hesitance on the subject, Sheryl carefully hung the dress up in the closet and sat on the corner of the bed. "Didn't it go well? They couldn't have *not* liked you, Meka. You're terrific."

"Actually, they seemed crazy about me." Meka glanced up with wide eyes. "His mom hinted to me that I'm exactly what she would look for in a daughter-in-law."

"Wow. In front of Ty?"

"No, but I think they said something similar to him."

"And did that make things awkward between the two of you?" No couple needed extra pressure to hasten to the altar. Then again, how awkward could things be if Meka had been staying with Ty for the past seventy-two hours?

"Awkward? Uh-uh. The weekend was amazing," Meka confided, her voice breathy enough to convey all the unsaid specifics of what "amazing" entailed. "I just... I mean, you know I'm crazy about him. I love Tyler, and he loves me."

"But?"

"We both have budding careers and our own places, and things have been so perfect the way they're going. We hadn't talked china patterns or where we should live or how many kids we should have. Now I feel like we should, and to tell you the truth..."

"You're nervous?"

Meka nodded. "I guess I knew he was The One. I just hadn't thought past that yet, to actually getting married. To never dating again. To *him* meeting *my* family. Both sets of them. Marriages aren't quite as steady as they once were, you know, and I don't want to make a mistake."

They didn't talk about it much, but Sheryl knew Tameka's parents had gone through an ugly divorce when Meka was in high school. Sheryl had actually gone with Meka freshman year to her mom's second wedding. That marriage hadn't lasted, and Sheryl had often glimpsed Meka's uncertainty that the current third marriage would fare any better.

But Meka wasn't her mother. "You and Ty are perfect together," Sheryl said. "Everything is going to be great, you'll see. I'm talking *sickeningly* great, where all the people around you are green with envy."

"You think?"

"Absolutely."

Tameka stood, a sheepish expression on her face. "Jeez, excuse me while I have some sort of Lifetime Channel moment. I guess it's true what they say about people getting overly sentimental around the holidays."

"Not a problem. That's what I'm here for."

Arching a brow, Meka teasingly corrected, "*I* thought you were here to borrow my shoes. I'm pretending not to notice that new boot box in your closet."

"Do not open till X-mas."

"That's what I figured." Her roommate laughed. "But I think I have the perfect pair of heels to go with that red dress. Want to go check?"

Sheryl followed her roommate across the short hallway that separated their rooms, musing over Ty and Meka and matrimony. After feeling her life was "crowded" the past few years, Sheryl hadn't been in a rush to look for love. She'd gone out with guys when the occasion arose and found herself in a few relationships, Brad being the last of them. But she'd never really pined to be with a man or despaired of being alone.

At the moment, she craved solitude. Her older sister, Colleen, and her brother were both married, leaving Sheryl and her younger sister, Lisa, single. But Lisa had been dating the same guy for two years now. Did it mean Sheryl was selfish just because she wanted sole dominion of the remote? That she liked the idea of going into her own bathroom without ever having to wait on someone else?

Having a healthy respect for privacy and personal space does not necessarily mean selfish.

Roles reversed, Sheryl now sat on Meka's Monet-like comforter, swirled in soft, mottled colors that almost formed a picture, and watched as her friend dug through her closet for the shoes.

"Found them," Tameka declared triumphantly. "But before I hand them over, there's a catch."

"I'm not asking Jonathan Spencer to the party, or anyone else from Ty's firm," Sheryl said quickly. "This is more of a business engagement than a social one for me."

"I wasn't going to try to blackmail you into a date," Tameka said indignantly. Apparently, she drew the line at ambush and coercion. "Just answer a question for me."

"Okay."

Tameka rose from her kneeling position on the floor of the closet, a pair of sin-red heels dangling off her fingers from their straps. "Did you buy that dress for Nathan Hall?"

"I don't think it's his size," Sheryl said blandly. "And he didn't strike me as the cross-dressing type, but I suppose you never kn—"

"I think I just remembered that I need to wear these shoes Friday night."

Sheryl sighed. "No, I didn't buy the dress for Nathan. It was just one of those female moments, where you find the perfect outfit and have to own it."

Her friend regarded her for a moment, then handed over the shoes. "Well, after seeing the dress on you, I have to agree. It *is* perfect. I just thought... Call me crazy, but the way you've been talking about him, it sounded almost as though you were developing a, um, crush. Or something."

"A crush is something you get on a member of a boy

band when you're fourteen. I'm a little beyond my Dear Diary years."

Since her roommate didn't look fully convinced, Sheryl pressed on. "Besides, even if you manage to overlook the whole he's-my-nemesis situation, he may be dating someone already. Didn't I tell you that when Jonathan and I ran into him, he was with a gorgeous redhead?"

"Yeah. You did. Maybe I *am* crazy for imagining any kind of chemistry brewing between the two of you."

"If not crazy, then at least more desperate than I thought to see me with a guy. Really. Me and Nathan Hall?" Sheryl's attempted laugh was entirely unsuccessful.

Eager to redirect the subject, she put on the borrowed shoes and stood, marveling once again at her luck in having a roommate with the same foot size. "Good call, Meka. These are going to be fabulous."

Tameka smiled. "Well, if he does bring that gorgeous redhead to the party…trust me, in that dress, you'll give her a run for her money."

Great. So Sheryl hadn't managed to convince herself *or* her roommate that she wasn't interested in the cynical columnist. But that's what denial was for.

AFTER HANDING her keys to the valet, Sheryl made the short walk between the curb and the entrance, huddling into her long coat and keeping her pace brisk. Not only was it freezing out here, the falling sleet was possibly wreaking havoc with her curled hair.

Stepping inside the front door, she was met by warm air and a friendly coat checker. The interior of the restaurant was an entirely different universe, one that moved slower and with more grace. Gone were the hostile weather and sounds of traffic. The lighting was subdued but not dim, and the focus of the lobby was a beautiful saltwater fish tank that took up most of one wall.

Overhead, tranquil music with an Oriental flair trickled through the speakers. Even the fragrance of the place soothed the nerves—ginger and sandalwood and whispers of other aromas that teased the senses without overwhelming.

After discarding her coat, she approached the front podium and asked a stately silver-haired Asian man with a completely unlined face if he could direct her to the room Brad had reserved for the night. The host led her past a wide open area housing a sushi bar, then pulled back a slatted bamboo divider to reveal a private back room. Several of her colleagues had already arrived and were drinking saki and exchanging Christmas jokes.

They sat on plump cushions around several huge rectangular "tables" that were part stove and part eating surface. Later, specially trained teppanyaki chefs would cook the food in front of them on the metal tabletop grills. And unfortunately, Sheryl noticed, her co-workers were observing tradition and had already removed their shoes. *Note to self—wearing the perfect pair of sexy red pumps is more effective if you go to a restaurant where you actually get to keep them on.*

Wyce Brown, HGS's vice president and one of its older employees, looked up with an approving grin. "Sheryl! Hey, you clean up real good."

She laughed and exchanged greetings with his wife. Next to the Browns sat Lilian Scheft from marketing and Denise Avery, both unaccompanied for the moment. But Denise, eye-catching tonight in a gold lamé blouse, had confided earlier in the week that she'd met a man through a dating service who planned to meet her here. Sheryl didn't place much stock in services paid to pair people off, but she mentally crossed her fingers for the cheery, kindhearted receptionist anyway.

Tall, elegant Lilian, on the other hand, was rarely seen with an escort and didn't need one. The marketing director always seemed very comfortable in her own skin. A talented find for HGS, the smart, confident woman managed to balance friends and privacy. She had dates when she wanted them, but didn't depend on anyone else to fulfill or entertain her. Sheryl realized with a start that Lilian was basically her role model.

A pretty kimono-clad waitress with jet-black hair in a braided bun appeared, collecting drink orders from those who were just arriving. Sheryl requested a glass of water with lemon as she waved to co-workers at other tables, including her assistant Grace who was giggling and finger-feeding California rolls to her hunk-of-the-month. Where did she consistently find guys who looked like that?

Denise's theory was that Grace must hang around in the parking lot of modeling agencies to meet them.

Sheryl also said hi to a few guys from accounting and poor Elliot Loomis, a young genius on the program development staff known for his bad luck with the ladies. He'd helped Brad refine the *Xandria* concept and had been assigned lead developer for the game. As if the suit over *Xandria Quest* wasn't enough to bum the kid out around the holidays, everyone in the office knew he had a raging crush on Grace.

After registering who was present and introducing

herself to a few spouses and dates she didn't know, Sheryl did a quick second scan, verifying the first thing she'd noticed. Nathan Hall wasn't here. She should feel relieved that he hadn't beaten her here and was already interviewing people with the aid of careful questions and a miniature tape recorder. Yet the nebulous emotion that rustled through her was more like disappointment.

She sat with Lilian and Denise, and the three of them compared notes on advertised weekend sales. But Sheryl only half listened, her eyes shooting to the wooden room divider each time she heard footsteps on the other side.

Denise nudged her with an elbow. "You waiting on someone, hon?"

"What?" Sheryl blinked. "Oh, no. Just surprised that Brad isn't here yet, this being his party."

"I think he had a meeting with Mark tonight to discuss settlement options," Lilian offered.

Denise ignored the explanation and continued to study Sheryl. "Sure you're just looking for Brad? You seem sort of flushed and... Well, you seem like me, and I'm waiting for someone I hope is my dream guy."

Lilian's thin, perfectly shaped eyebrows shot skyward as she did a double take in Sheryl's direction. "You and Brad aren't rekindling the old flame, are you?"

"No! Of course not." To be honest, in a corporate environment such as the one HGS was finally achieving, Sheryl wouldn't normally dream of dating her boss. It had just been something that happened, back when the structure of the company had been casual and young.

An expressive person, Brad sometimes threw his arm around Sheryl or called her sweetie at the office.

She was sensitive to it since they did share a past, but the truth was, he was just as likely to hug Dean from accounting if the man told him they'd had a profitable year.

That anyone could suspect a man who ran his company like a benevolent camp counselor of stealing anything was ludicrous. For the first time, she wondered if maybe inviting Nathan Hall to this party was a good idea after all. Maybe he'd spend a couple of hours with her affable employer and decide Kendra Mathers was clearly mistaken.

"Well, there's my date," Denise said with yet another exuberant nudge to Sheryl's side. Sheryl made a note to find a different seat for dinner. A couple of hours of this, and she'd have to go to the emergency room to have her ribs taped afterwards.

An unfamiliar man with rumpled hair and wire-rim glasses stood at the head of the room, scanning it nervously.

"That's Joe," Denise gushed. "He e-mailed me his picture, but he's even cuter in person!"

Sheryl stood immediately to give the newcomer her place, waving him over. Though that seemed suddenly unnecessary given Denise's shrill, *"Yoo-hoo, Joe! Over here!"*

Behind the now-startled Joe, Sheryl caught sight of her boss and excused herself. Maybe it was the holiday spirit making her more gracious, but she wanted to tell him that she was sorry she'd protested his recent decisions and that maybe inviting Nathan Hall hadn't been a bad idea. She stepped around the bamboo screen partitioning off the room and waited as Brad finished talking to the restaurant manager.

Her employer's blue eyes widened at the sight of her. "Wow."

"Thanks."

He pulled her into a quick hug and kissed her cheek. "No, I mean, *wow*, Sheryl. You're more gorgeous than ever tonight. And that's saying something."

She leaned back, preparing to politely downplay his excessive flattery, when she glimpsed the dark figure coming down the hallway.

"Am I interrupting something?" Nathan asked, his voice holding more chill than the arctic front scheduled to move in tonight.

Startled by Nathan's sudden appearance, she quickly lurched away from Brad. "N-no."

Too late, she realized that her springing away and loss of composure might make her appear guilty of something. *Of what?* an inner voice scoffed. Hugging an old friend Merry Christmas could hardly qualify as a sex scandal, even to a suspicious reporter trying to manufacture a story.

Squaring her shoulders and plastering a smile on her face, she told Brad, "This, of course, is Nathan Hall, the *Sojourner*'s esteemed columnist. Mr. Hall, my boss, Brad Hammond."

Nathan's gaze simmered on her a moment longer before he turned to shake Brad's hand. "Mr. Hammond. I appreciate your hospitality tonight."

The two men made small talk and even though it had been her plan to carefully monitor Brad's words tonight and discreetly redirect conversation if Nathan tried to lead him toward any verbal land mines, Sheryl was barely listening. But, boy, she was *looking*. Not a single bell in sight, Nathan wore a dressy turtleneck sweater of the darkest, deepest brown, over slacks a lighter shade of cinnamon.

The sweater's high neck emphasized the chiseled cut of his jaw and handsome face, while the thickly knit fabric stretched lovingly across his strong chest and shoulders. In the rich chocolate color, he looked like something to be savored with whipped cream.

Though he was still chatting with Brad about the expected weather this evening, Nathan's gaze flickered to her for a moment, somehow knowing. He couldn't possibly guess she was standing there thinking how— *yummy, edible, I want!*—attractive he was. Could he?

Her face warmed, and she stepped between the two men, temporarily insuring that Nathan couldn't clearly see her expression. Heaven knew what kind of guilt, desire or embarrassment he might read in her eyes.

"Mr. Hammond," she instructed Brad, "you might want to go inside now so you have some time to mingle before dinner starts."

Brad nodded and shook Nathan's hand again. "Sheryl, save a spot next to us for Mr. Hall. He's my guest of honor tonight."

"Of course," she said, wishing she could sit at the opposite end of the table from Nathan, her planned vigilance for the evening be darned, and join the people she'd seen earlier enjoying saki.

We'll call vigilance Plan A and saki Plan B. No question which sounded better. Unfortunately, there was also no question of which course she would follow, and it didn't involve the potent Japanese rice wine.

Pushing aside the lightweight room divider, Brad entered the private dining room. Sheryl wanted to scurry in after him and introduce Nathan to everyone she knew by name. For that matter, if it helped her campaign to keep the columnist busy with small talk, she'd use tonight to meet those she didn't know. The last thing she wanted was for him to have a long and meaningful conversation with anyone at HGS.

But she'd already jerked away from Brad as though Nathan had caught them plotting something and then stared at the journalist with salacious interest. Now, it was about time she took a deliberate moment to project a collected, unflappable image.

She paused purposefully, giving them the chance to be alone. Her subliminal way of saying *You don't scare me*. Made her mouth go dry and her hormones sing raucous love songs, maybe, but he didn't scare her.

"I'm glad you could join us this evening, Mr. Hall. I'm sure you have a busy schedule of your own, and it was kind of you to work us in on such short notice."

Unexpectedly, he reached out to tip her chin up with his index finger. That single place where their bodies connected sent heat whirling through her. The way he locked gazes with her, searching her eyes, did nothing to quell the dizzying sensation.

"Glad to see me, huh?" He quirked an eyebrow.

Taking a measured step back—refusing to actually give the appearance of fleeing—she said brightly, "I should have made it clear the invitation was for two. You could have invited your friend. Kaylee, right?" *Excellent job, Sher. You sound completely unaffected by his touch.* Who knew she was capable of such an Oscar-worthy performance?

Nathan studied her a second, as though debating his next words, then shrugged. "I didn't want to cut into her limited time with her husband since he's actually off duty tonight."

"Sh-she's married?"

He nodded, a slight smile on his face. "She and her husband, Frank, are the closest thing I have to family in Seattle."

"Oh."

For a moment, her mind blanked out everything but the intense relief she felt. So he wasn't in a relationship with the inhumanly gorgeous woman? Thoughts jumbled, she decided that now would be a good time to join the others.

"We should go in," she said, hoping she still sounded composed.

"After you." But he stopped her with a light hand on her bared shoulder, a whisper of a touch that slid away from her skin as suddenly as the contact had registered. "By the way, nice dress."

The sensual appreciation in his gaze left her too breathless to voice a response, which was probably just as well. It kept her from soliciting his opinion on how she looked out of the dress.

6

NATHAN LEANED BACK slightly, allowing room for the waitress who was distributing delicate bowls of salad next to each person's tiny trio of prefilled sauce dishes. Beside him, Sheryl toyed with her salad, but she didn't seem any more interested in food than Nathan was.

She looked incredible tonight, so incredible he'd had to force himself not to stare when she'd sat down on the cushion next to him. The hem of her unforgettable red dress had slid teasingly up her silky legs, not revealing anything indecent, just whetting his appetite to see more.

He hadn't been surprised that she'd managed to seat herself between him and the boss she seemed so protective of, but Nathan had been completely poleaxed by the jealousy he'd felt when Brad squeezed her hand a few minutes ago. Sheryl hadn't looked happy about the gesture herself. Was she suffering from an employer's unwanted attentions? No, that didn't make sense, given her ultraloyal defense of him. Besides, she didn't seem the type to be quietly victimized by sexual harassment.

So, given Brad's affection toward her and the embrace Nathan had walked in on when he arrived...had Nathan's idle suspicion the other day in the *Sojourner* office been correct? *Was* there something romantic going on between Sheryl and Hammond? Maybe the irritation that had crossed her face when Brad hugged her wasn't because she was annoyed with Brad himself, but because she wanted to be discreet when it came to an office romance.

If Sheryl's loyalty to her job wasn't incentive enough for her to turn a blind eye toward shady practices, was love?

Of course, there was always the possibility that she truly believed Hammond had been wrongly accused. And as long as he was playing devil's advocate, there was a *chance* Hammond actually was innocent. Nathan didn't buy that, but his conscience was apparently caught up in that whole till-proven-guilty technicality.

"And for you, sir?"

He was jerked from his thoughts by the waitress's lilting voice as she collected orders so that the chefs would have the necessary ingredients for each meal.

"Oh, steak and scallops," he told the patient young woman.

As the waitress bustled off, Brad leaned partially across Sheryl, wanting to talk more about *Xandria Quest*.

"Did I tell you about how I got the idea for the 'snow-warths' on level nine?" the man asked. His face lit up like an overdecorated Christmas tree.

Nathan shook his head. "I think we only covered how you came up with every idea for levels one through eight."

Sheryl glared, but his sarcasm seemed lost on her employer, who launched into an explanation of what a "warth" was and what fictional weaponry was needed in the game to kill one.

This was exactly the type of thing Nathan had expected tonight. In theory, Brad's ability to explain how and why each facet of the game was developed was a good defense against the claim that he'd stolen part or all of the premise from Kendra Mathers. On the other hand, it all seemed a little too pat. Invite Nathan here and then pepper him with anecdotes that pointed to Brad's innocence? As if a smart man wouldn't have spent the entire week planning what he'd say. Hammond could have been diligently fabricating convincing stories from the moment Sheryl relayed Nathan's acceptance.

As Brad paused for a breath, no doubt gearing up to explain the complexities of level ten, Sheryl turned to Nathan. "How's your food?"

But Brad answered, "We're only on the salad, Sheryl, and his is the same as yours. Wait until the chefs come in, that's when things really get good. Now, in addition to 'warths' are the 'gargunds'..."

Nathan almost laughed at the irony of the situation. When Sheryl had first escorted him into the room, she'd smoothly played hostess, steering Nathan around the room and introducing him to people. She'd even scowled at one bubbly blond woman whose attitude had altered drastically when she'd realized he was *that* Nathan Hall. Sheryl had explained that Nathan was Hammond's guest of honor tonight, and no one was to let any differences of opinion spoil the evening. Despite her near-defense of him, Nathan noticed that she kept him circulating, unable to engage in any meaningful, investigative conversation.

But the one person she hadn't been able to keep Nathan from was Brad himself. Because Hammond sought Nathan out at every turn, refusing to let Sheryl get a word in edgewise in spite of her strategic seating between the two men.

Brad had explained in detail, sounding very much like an infomercial, that with so many games on the market, his stood out because of its character depth and intricate plot. As well as offering the average PC player something different from racing or shoot-'em-up games, Brad had made a huge hit with the fantasy and computer enthusiasts who held actual public tournaments where games like *Xandria Quest* were becoming this generation's technologically advanced Dungeons & Dragons.

Though Brad was clearly going out of his way to show he was a man with nothing to hide, Nathan trusted the software mogul—future mogul, anyway—even less now. The man was just *too* nice. He had a wide-eyed, aw-shucks demeanor you didn't see much anymore. At least, not outside farming communities in the rural Midwest. The only people who worked that hard at being sincere were politicians, televangelists and used-car salesmen.

Surely Sheryl had better taste in men than *that?*

The man on the other side of Brad, Vice President Wyce Brown, suddenly captured Hammond's attention and liberated Nathan from further conversation. He considered offering to name his firstborn Wyce.

Next to him, Sheryl relaxed, too, her graceful shoulders rolling forward slightly as she exhaled deeply. Brad seemed to think he and Nathan were now buddies, but she'd been more responsive to Nathan's veiled sarcasm. Did she know her boss was digging a hole for himself?

Please tell me she isn't with this guy.

Background information on Kendra Mathers showed she was a struggling writer who'd won some awards, but not found her publishing break, had no connections to Hammond or inside information, and no history of filing lawsuits, frivolous or otherwise. On the other hand, Brad Hammond was an ambitious man, and very likely a phony. Nathan hated to see Sheryl with someone like that. Even if Brad actually *was* innocent, Nathan didn't like the thought of them together.

Despite the growing certainty that his speculation had nothing to do with reporter's curiosity, Nathan couldn't refrain from asking, "So what about your date?"

Sheryl's head whipped around, the sweet undertones of her tangy perfume making his insides clench. Bad enough that she looked that good, did she have to smell like a living, breathing fantasy?

"I'm sorry," she said. "What did you ask? I'm not sure I heard right."

His question probably did seem random to her, since she couldn't know he'd spent the entire salad course wondering about her taste in men and whether or not she was single. "You asked about Kaylee earlier. It made me think of your date at the theater. What was his name?"

"Jonathan. Jonathan Spencer, but he was more of an acquaintance than a date. A friend of a friend who had an extra ticket."

"And he inflicted the ticket on you?"

She laughed. "Definitely the worst ballet I've ever seen."

Watching her, he wished he had more reasons to make her smile. But the father who had raised him alone after Nathan's mother abandoned them both had had plenty to say about bending your personal code to make a woman happy. Though following HGS's lawsuit didn't exactly carry global repercussions or a chance at the Pulitzer, Nathan still wouldn't be able to look himself in the eye if he eased off Brad just because Sheryl had a nice smile.

"So Jonathan isn't your boyfriend?" Dumb to frame a question she'd already answered, but keeping the conversation going gave him something to do besides stare at her mouth and wonder if it was as tartly sweet as her perfume.

"I'm single," she blurted. And as though concerned her quick admission sounded like an invitation, she added, "I like it that way. Answering to no one but myself."

If she were involved romantically with Brad, would she have admitted it? Nathan wanted to feel relief at her words, but wasn't sure it was safe to yet.

Instead he only said, "Yeah, I'm a fan of the single life, too." It had its pluses. You never had to worry that someone was lying. Or getting ready to leave you.

At that moment, several chefs in red jackets and straight black hats entered the room, wheeling large carts of food, sauces and spices. The tall chef closest to Nathan stepped behind their table, greeting everyone and checking to make sure he had the correct orders. He heated the grill then poured oil across the metal surface.

Nathan identified with the resulting sizzle. It was what he felt every time the woman next to him glanced in his direction.

Around the table, people watched in appreciative awe as the chef artistically sliced and diced a mixture of vegetables for the fried rice, then tossed eggs into the air and behind his back before catching and cracking them perfectly on the hot surface. He pitched the empty shells heavenward where they landed effort-lessly in the recessed top of his hat.

Sheryl clapped along with her companions after the egg display, but Nathan noticed that she flinched when the chef began juggling two wickedly sharp knives.

Unable to pass up the opportunity to lean closer to her, he murmured teasingly, "I'm sure the man knows what he's doing, still... Hammond gets you guys good health insurance, right?"

"He takes care of us." She pursed her lips. "But I'm more concerned about leaving with the same number of fingers I arrived with than I am about my deduct-ible."

He chuckled.

As the chef used a spatula to flip grilled shrimp ap-petizers on to everyone's plates around the table, Sheryl studied Nathan's smile, making him feel self-conscious.

"What?" he asked finally.

"I was just wondering if you were having a good time," she said.

How to answer that? "The food's wonderful." With his pair of chopsticks, he lifted a piece of shrimp, low-ered it into one of the spicy dips the waitress had set out, then plopped it into his mouth without tasting it at all.

"And the company?"

Alarmingly sexy. "They seem nice enough. Normal. It's not like I expected to walk into the room and find green people with horns and forked tongues, Sheryl." He hadn't meant to use her first name. *Ms. Dayton* was a nice barrier.

Ignoring the slip, he continued, "But if you think I'm going to run right out and stop the presses saying that

Hammond can't possibly be guilty of anything just because I met a few people who seemed like decent folks, you're nuts."

She made a frustrated sound in her throat. Maybe because calling a woman nuts wasn't the way to win her heart.

I don't want her heart. Nonetheless, as he heard his next sentence leave his mouth, he wondered if he were trying to mollify her and why he would do that. "But you don't have to worry about any scathing columns coming from my word processor right now."

Her eyes widened. "Does that mean you won't be writing about us anymore?"

"There's nothing *to* write, at the moment. I'm sorry, but two sets of lawyers trying to reach an out-of-court settlement isn't all that gripping. Unless something new comes up—"

"Columnists are allowed to use opinions, though, right? I mean you do more than just straight articles. If you—"

He headed her off before she said something to really anger him. "Just because you guys are buying me dinner, don't expect me to say it's my opinion that Kendra Mathers is full of it."

"Of course not! I just meant that if after a little further research…"

Brad leaned around from the other side of Sheryl, frowning at their low, tense voices. "You two are talking shop, aren't you?"

"Wasn't that the idea?" Nathan countered. "To get me here so that I could hear your side of it?"

"That sounds so…" The other man shrugged. "I don't really have a *side*. I was just running my company, minding my own business, when this pesky lawsuit cropped up. But I'm sure it'll all work out."

Didn't the man even know how he sounded? Just minding my own business? The only thing he could do to affect a more clichéd image of innocence would be to look up at the sky with his hands clasped behind his back and whistle.

"Yeah," Nathan drawled, "you gotta hate those darn pesky lawsuits."

He had met lots of people in the course of his job, interviewed and profiled them. Less than five percent of those people were as sentimental and earnest as Brad Hammond and genuine to boot. *None* of them ran businesses in competitive fields. What were the odds the guy was for real? Brad and his fledgling upstart company had been the focus of a number of human interest pieces, but did the public know the actual man or was Hammond feeding them a do-gooder image no more valid than a certain red-nosed reindeer who was able to fly?

Despite what he'd said about the story essentially being cold, Nathan wanted to investigate further. His renewed efforts wouldn't endear him to Sheryl any, but why should that matter? Nathan wasn't someone who let personal feelings interfere with the truth. Not that he had feelings for her, he assured himself.

Attraction, sure. But there was no way he'd ever let it become anything deeper.

"Okay, so what are we doing tomorrow night?"

Tameka and Ty glanced up from their cuddled position on the sofa, where they were watching *It's A Wonderful Life*. To say they looked surprised by

Sheryl's unorthodox entrance would be an understatement.

"Hello to you, too," Meka said, as Tyler echoed, "Tomorrow?" in a perplexed tone. He sounded like a man who feared he'd forgotten prearranged plans and wasn't sure yet how much trouble he'd be in for the memory lapse.

Sheryl closed the front door she'd all but thrown open, and shrugged out of her coat. "You mentioned we'd do some double-dating. Hang out, the four of us." Whoever the heck the unknown fourth was. "Tomorrow's Saturday, and I'm free if you guys are. And if you know a fourth."

Good grief, she sounded like her mom trying to find someone to round out a bridge night.

"You look great," Ty interjected, still wearing his hope-I'm-not-in-trouble expression. "New dress?"

Sheryl nodded. In retrospect, she should have skipped the killer dress and gone with full body armor. Nathan had barely touched her tonight, but even the smallest brush of his hand against exposed skin had sent shivers of need through her. How could she respond so strongly to a guy she barely knew?

What's to know? He's hot, funny, successful, principled. Hot. He has the good sense not to enjoy bad experimental theater, and did I mention he's hot?

It had been a long time since Brad, and that hadn't exactly been a passionate relationship. So maybe her unwanted reactions to Nathan were magnified because there was no other guy in her life. Solution: find a guy. Quickly!

She'd never jump into bed with someone to avoid fantasizing about being in bed with Nathan, of course, but she could at least spend a Saturday night on a date. If Tameka and Ty could produce one.

Meka straightened, zapping the remote control in the direction of the television and ending Jimmy Stewart's heartfelt monologue. "You sure about this?"

"It was your idea, remember?" Sheryl dropped into the battered recliner her father had given her when he got his new easy chair for his birthday. Meka was forever insisting they slipcover the thing—or burn it. "You wanted me to meet a few guys, spend more 'fun couple time' with you and Ty. I told you that I was up for it, but short of one regrettable evening of ballet—"

Ty laughed. "Yeah, Jonathan seems psychologically scarred by the performance. I think he's stopped speaking to the guy who gave him the tickets in the first place."

Meka ignored her boyfriend's aside. "You *reluctantly* agreed to my suggestion, but now you seem suspiciously enthusiastic. What happened tonight?"

"It was a business dinner at a Japanese restaurant," Sheryl hedged. "We ate with chopsticks and exchanged Secret Santa gifts. Nothing earth-shattering." Unless you counted the way she felt when Nathan looked at her.

Disregarding the possibility of a hormone-induced overactive imagination, there had been one moment tonight when she could have sworn he'd wanted to kiss her. She'd laughed at something he'd said—was it fair for one guy to be sexy *and* amusing?—and his gaze had dropped to her mouth.

That's when genuine panic had set in. So far, they'd been butting heads over his stubborn cynicism, but if that were to change, if he directed the full force of his charm at her—

"I'd melt like ice cream under hot fudge," she muttered.

"What did you just say?" Meka demanded.

"Nothing."

Ty rubbed his stomach. "Sounded like she mentioned ice cream. You guys have any?" When neither of them answered, he rose and padded to the kitchen to check for himself.

Meka lowered her voice to just above a whisper. "You want to tell me what this is really about?"

No.

"He had that Kaylee woman with him, didn't he?" Meka guessed.

"Uh-uh. He showed up alone. Seems to be as single as I am, we both agreed that we like our solitude."

Meka snorted. "Says the woman begging me to help her find a date for tomorrow."

Not *begging*. Pleading, perhaps.

"That's different," Sheryl protested. "I'm not looking for someone who knows how to make my coffee in the morning, just a guy whose company we can all appreciate for a few hours to have a fun double date. It was your idea."

Meka mulled it over, presumably scanning her internal address book for someone suitable.

Sheryl bit her lip as a thought struck her. "I should have asked first what you and Ty's plans were. Sorry." She hadn't meant to be so self-absorbed...though Nathan-absorbed was more accurate.

"No problem," Meka said. "After seeing his parents last weekend and all the holiday craziness coming up, we were planning to lie low. An evening out with a foursome actually sounds pretty good for unwinding. A casual dinner with friends."

"Right, that's all I want."

Though she still looked skeptical about her roommate's ulterior motives, Meka nodded in sudden decision. "I stay in touch with a guy I took design classes with. Dane. He and his girlfriend broke up about a month ago, so he might be free. Getting out could be just what he needs right now. I'll bet the two of you hit it off, and Ty's met him before. I'll e-mail Dane tonight. Maybe we can even go to Grungy's after dinner, shoot some pool and listen to live music."

"Thanks." An evening out would keep Sheryl from sitting at home, pretending to watch sitcom reruns while in reality, fixating on Nathan Hall. She supposed she could hit the malls—only twelve shopping days left, after all. But the last time she'd gone gift-hunting while preoccupied with Nathan, she'd ended up with a bright red dress that could have paid for presents for her combined siblings.

Sheryl let her mind take her back to that moment when Nathan had reached out to caress her shoulder, his eyes warm with masculine appreciation.

Nice dress.

Who was she kidding? The tone of his voice alone had been worth the price she'd paid.

7

IT TOOK ALL DAY Sunday to get the tuneless pounding of Saturday night's bass-heavy music out of her head, but by the time Sheryl reached work Monday morning, her hearing had returned to normal. Despite progress on the auditory front, however, the caffeine count in her blood was dangerously low. Stopping by her office only long enough to toss her purse and coat inside, she skipped straight to the breakroom without even pausing to boot up her computer.

When she discovered that other nonmorning individuals had already drained the last of the high-test stuff without bothering to put on another pot, an involuntary growl emitted from her throat. The decaf pitcher was full, of course, but what was the point of that?

Behind her, someone made a startled sound, and she glanced over her shoulder to find Elliot Loomis pushing his glasses up on the bridge of his nose and looking nervous.

"This is a bad time," he said, not making it a question.

"'Course not." She'd just assumed she was alone while she mentally throttled whoever hadn't refilled the coffeepot. "I was about to make more java. Want a cup?"

He edged past her, his eyes on the floor, then lifted

the decaf pitcher. "No, thanks, I drink this. Caffeine makes me jittery."

Huh? A foreign concept to her, but she'd heard rumors it could do that to people. And Elliot especially didn't need to be any shakier.

Brad had told her more than once how Elliot was a techie genius with a fertile imagination for their games, an employee who would eventually do great things for the company. But as gifted as Elliot was with computers, he was equally nongifted with people. Though Brad didn't show any outward favoritism to the awkward young man who had graduated college quite early, Sheryl suspected that her boss saw a lot of himself in the not-yet-confident boy genius. This morning Elliot seemed even more painfully shy than normal.

Probably your fault. He caught you in a feral, precoffee mode, telepathically stringing up co-workers. She'd most likely set the kid back months in social courage.

"Ms. Dayton?"

"Sheryl, please."

"Right. Sh-Sheryl. I was wondering if, um..."

She smiled reassuringly, hoping the nonverbal encouragement would get him going again.

Lowering his gaze, he tugged nervously at the hem of his beige shirt. Elliot wore a lot of beige.

So much for nonverbal. "Is there something I can do for you, Elliot?"

He glanced up, gratitude shining in his green eyes. "I hope so. I was wondering if you'd consent to—"

Oh, no. He wasn't going to ask her out, was he? They were definitely mismatched, but she wasn't sure she had it in her to turn the kid down and further dent his self-esteem.

"—put in a good word for me?" he finished hopefully.

He must mean with her assistant, Grace, Sheryl realized belatedly, feeling like an arrogant fool. Duh.

Before she could answer the anxiously waiting
young man, Denise bustled into the breakroom. "Good
morning, people!" A bona fide morning person, the receptionist usually sounded like a drill sergeant on up-
pers any time before noon. A maniacally cheerful ma-
rine. "How was everyone's weekend?"

Elliot shot Sheryl a glance that she instantly interpreted
as a request for silence. He'd been nervous enough about
discussing his feelings for Grace without an audience.
She winked at him in a your-secret's-safe-with-me
expression, though it might have resembled a my-
contact-dried-out-and-is-stuck-to-my-retina expression—
Sheryl wasn't typically much of a winker.

Getting no takers, Denise went ahead and answered
her own question. "*My* weekend was unbelievable."
The way she sighed at the end of her sentence caused
Sheryl to take a second look at the blond thirty-
something.

Sure enough, Denise appeared even happier than
usual today. Easy to see how one might have had difficulty telling the difference.

Sheryl's female intuition clicked, more accurate this
time than when she'd suspected Elliot of wanting to
ask her out. "Joe?"

Denise exhaled another dreamy sigh as she dropped
into one of the plastic green chairs. "Joe! He's so kind.
Sort of quiet, but what a good listener. He just let me go
on and on! You might not have noticed this, but I can
be a nervous talker. Fortunately, he said he didn't
mind at all, that he doesn't usually know what to say

when he meets a woman and was fascinated—fascinated!—by all my stories." With a twinkle in her eyes, she added, "And he's a damn good kisser."

Elliot blushed and glanced at the door as though calculating his personal best sprint time.

Sheryl caught his eye. "Why don't you try to stop by my office later today, and we'll continue our conversation, okay?"

He nodded gratefully, then beat a hasty retreat.

Once he was gone, Sheryl checked her watch. Deciding she could take a few extra minutes, she sat in a chair next to Denise, who was obviously dying to spill the details of her romantic weekend.

"Okay," Sheryl encouraged. "Let's hear all about it."

Denise launched into such a comprehensive accounting of her time with Joe that Sheryl quickly realized she should have chosen her wording more carefully. Maybe, *let's have a summary of the highlights.* But at least dating was going well for *someone.*

Sheryl's double date on Saturday had started out all right. Dane was funny, charming and undeniably good-looking. But not even those qualities had been able to stop her from unintentionally comparing him to Nathan. Then a definite pall had fallen over the evening when the band at Grungy's slowed down long enough to play what had apparently been "the song" for Dane and his ex-girlfriend. As though he were an uncorked bottle, he'd talked about her nonstop from that point on.

The fact that he was more interested in an old flame than in Sheryl actually made her feel less guilty for her preoccupation with Nathan. She'd originally thought a major perk of Meka's dating plan would be to take her mind off the opinionated columnist. It wasn't working, though, and it was unfair to her dates in the meantime.

Which meant she needed to come up with a new way to exorcise him from her system, the sooner the better.

NATHAN BLINKED at his computer screen, aware that he'd dimly heard keys clicking but had no idea what he'd just typed. He reread his last sentence on a proposed public school policy change and groaned. *That* was the best he'd been able to come up with? If the rest of the column was as bad, the page it was printed on wouldn't be fit to line a birdcage.

But he couldn't concentrate this morning. When he'd come in an hour ago, he'd left a message on Beth's desk, asking to see the intern as soon as she arrived. Though standard background checks had already been run on Brad Hammond, Nathan wanted to ask Beth if she had time to do a little more digging, just in case something had been overlooked. Naturally, thoughts of Hammond Gaming Software had led to Sheryl, and with the amount of work he'd managed to do so far, he might as well have taken the day off.

He tried blinking in rapid succession this time to clear his mind, but erasing the mental picture of Sheryl was impossible. Not that it mattered much, he supposed. The weekend had proven his imagination was qualified—correction, eager—to constantly provide new images. Some more suited to an adult magazine than a family newspaper.

Even his seemingly innocuous thoughts...weren't. Simply recalling her smile, *especially* recalling her smile, was enough to accelerate his pulse. Her humor and intelligence were as attractive as her figure; Nathan liked smart women. Passion, another irresistible quality, expressed itself in many forms. Remembering the jade fire in her eyes when she was riled made him wonder what kissing her would be like. Most of all, though, it was her loyalty that not only tugged at his heartstrings but tied them into elaborate knots.

When she spoke in defense of Brad Hammond, she was fierce. Nathan might believe her opinion was dead wrong and misguided, but how could he condemn her for having the one quality he'd spent his adolescence wishing his mother had possessed? Devotion.

The phone rang curtly, and Nathan jumped.

Rather than be annoyed by the intrusion, as he would have been had the caller interrupted actual writing, he was grateful for the distraction.

Lifting the receiver, he answered, "*Seattle Sojourner*. Nathan Hall speaking."

"The same Nathan Hall who wrote about Brad Hammond and the suit against him?" a woman asked, punctuating her question with a nervous laugh.

Nathan resisted a groan at the universe's joke on him. Of all the reasons for his phone to ring, this had to be about Sheryl's company?

"I did do a few columns on the subject." He wondered why anyone outside of Hammond Gaming Software would bother calling him about it now.

"I have some information about Brad Hammond I believe you'll find interesting." A note of predatory expectation crept into her gravelly voice. Hard to tell if the husky edge came from a cold, age or a pack-a-day habit.

"And you are?" Nathan wanted to know. He was hardly going to get excited about random information from an unidentified caller who didn't sound remotely objective about the topic. A "deep throat" character might fly in bad movies-of-the-week, but Nathan's editors were touchy about things like unverifiable sources.

"I'm not ready to reveal my name just yet," the woman said melodramatically. "But would it interest you to know that Brad Hammond has been accused of theft before?"

Aha! Nathan's sense of righteous indignation flared. All his instincts told him the guy was a fraud, and now maybe someone was offering proof. But who the someone was remained a critical question. Sometimes an old classmate or vengeful ex-girlfriend saw a name they recognized in the papers and later remembered a past anecdote, like Brad had been suspected of stealing someone's lunch money in high school.

Rare but not unheard of, those calls were almost always motivated by petty personal grudges or a desire for a little attention, not civic duty or an interest in accurate journalism.

This call, however, quickly proved to be motivated by greed. "If I knew something, what would it be worth to you?" she asked coyly.

"You think I'm going to *pay* you?" Nathan said incredulously, his faith in her credibility slipping another notch.

He grinned despite himself as he looked around his tiny office and sat back in his defective chair. Whoever his mystery caller was, she had a skewed perception of the newspaper's budget. She also had a pretty obvious ulterior motive for calling. Although, he supposed it wasn't "ulterior" if one flat-out demanded cash in return for the tip.

"It could be your big break," she added when she realized he wasn't pouncing on her offer. Desperation added to the melodrama of her tone.

His big break? Even if Hammond was found guilty, ordered by the court to pay huge compensatory damages to plaintiff Kendra Mathers and subsequently went out of business, Nathan doubted it would take the Associated Press by storm. He planned to investigate Hammond further, but not by shelling out money to a woman who sounded more like a flake the longer this conversation continued.

"Ma'am, I'm afraid you have the *Sojourner* confused with the tabloids. Happy holidays."

He hung up the phone amid her objections, staring sightlessly into space for a moment before turning back to his computer. Instead of simply highlighting and deleting his last sentence, he took his frustration out on the backspace key.

Why not just go ahead and erase everything after his byline? Because, frankly, nothing he'd written today was worth reading.

Picking up the legal pad on his desk, he flipped to a page of outdated personal reminders he'd left for himself. He ripped the sheet out with a satisfying *ffft*, wadded it into a pale yellow ball and shot a basket through the hoop over his garbage can. Subsequent pages of scribbled notes, as well as old memos, sailed through the air as he made basket after basket.

What information had the mystery caller been trying to get him to buy? And was it legitimate? If there were skeletons in Brad's closet, why hadn't they come out sooner, amid the good and bad publicity surrounding the software entrepreneur over the past year? Of course, if Nathan didn't believe those skeletons existed, why was he leaving notes for Beth, asking her to dig deeper into Hammond's past?

Questions tumbled through Nathan's mind with all the order and clarity of laundry in the dryer.

Great, now even my thoughts have turned to bad writing.

Just who was his caller, anyway? The obvious woman who would want to damage Brad's reputation was Kendra Mathers herself. But the pictures he'd seen of the young woman didn't gel with the gravelly voice of the caller. Besides, Kendra would have given her name. She'd sought publicity for herself and her case since filing the suit.

She seemed very determined that people know about how she'd been "violated." She'd talked about how it felt to create something, only to have it stolen from you. As a writer, even though he dealt with nonfiction, Nathan could empathize with her obvious anger. If she were telling the truth, Brad's crime must be doubly painful for her when she was limited to scattered short story sales and two Web site serials she'd had before *Xandria Quest* came out, while HGS raked in money off of holiday sales. Profiting from what was allegedly her unrecognized creative genius.

"This isn't getting me anywhere."

But maybe if Nathan were out actively researching, talking to the people who actually worked with Brad and might have insight into the man... Surely not everyone at his office adored him?

Sitting cooped up in this office certainly wasn't accomplishing anything. And hadn't Brad himself said Nathan was welcome anytime at Hammond Gaming Software, even offering to give him a tour of the place?

Nathan stood carefully. If one rose too quickly from

The Chair, the springs reacted to the pressure change by jolting forward and knocking an unsuspecting victim into the edge of the desk. Already punching buttons on his cell phone as he grabbed his coat, he got the number for HGS's office. He dialed en route to the elevator, hoping to catch Brad and take him up on his offered tour.

No doubt the second Sheryl heard Nathan was on the premises, she'd try to run interference between the two men, the way she'd unsuccessfully attempted to at the Christmas party. But his visit today was motivated by a tip on Brad's past. Wanting to see Sheryl didn't enter into it. Much.

8

SHERYL SHOOK HER HEAD adamantly even though she knew Meka couldn't see her over the phone. "No, I don't think that's such a good idea," she said in response to her roommate's offer to cook dinner tonight for Ty, Sheryl and Dane.

"I've already talked to Dane, and he's free," Meka said. "He really wishes Saturday night had gone better and wants to make it up to you. Come on, he's a great guy. Talented, sensitive, and even you said he was gorgeous... I like him so you'd never have to worry that your best friend and boyfriend don't get along. Give me one good reason why you wouldn't want a second date."

I'll take Obvious Answers for a thousand, Alex. "Um, because he's in love with someone else?"

Meka sighed. "No, he's not. I know he got a little nostalgic, but he assures me he's over that."

Then the man was kidding himself.

Sheryl recalled the depth of emotion in Dane's eyes as he'd waxed poetic about his ex. Had she ever felt that way about someone? She was tempted to wonder what it was like, but that level of feeling wasn't in keeping with her liking her independence. Not to mention, judging from the pain that had shadowed his movie-star-handsome features, emotion like that packed a hell of a risk.

"Sorry, Meka. Not interested." Until she was certain she'd worked Nathan Hall out of her system, no more substitutes.

"If you're going to be ridiculously picky, you'll wind up old and alone with a houseful of cats for company," Meka scolded.

"I'll chance it, but thanks."

"Look, just one meal. If things don't go well tonight, then—"

"I don't want to be curt, but the HGS Holiday Festival is Saturday." Sheryl glanced from her day-planner to her e-mail in-box, both of which were full of reminders of things she needed to do immediately. "Now isn't a great time to discuss this."

"You're right, I'm sorry." Meka strategically retreated. "Tell you what, you don't need to give me an answer now, anyway. We'll just talk about it tonight. Bye!"

Click.

Talk about it tonight? Ha! When? As Ty and Dane set the table for dinner while Sheryl helped Meka finish in the kitchen? *I'm on to you, Williams!*

Sheryl hung up the phone just as footsteps approached outside her office door. "Oh, good." She glanced up from her desk expectantly. "Did you get a chance to pick up those—"

The rest of her intended words evaporated in her throat like beads of moisture rising from the pavement on a long, hot summer day. Or maybe it was just that seeing Nathan made her think heat wave type thoughts.

"You're not Grace," she ventured.

"Not even particularly graceful," he said with mock regret. "I take it you expected someone else?"

"Well I certainly didn't expect you." Annoyed by her breathless tone, she crossed her arms over her chest and adopted a more flippant attitude. Shooting a cheeky grin in his direction, she added, "But I hope you didn't come to see me without an appointment because I'm very busy and important. You could always call and schedule something."

Nathan smirked at her smart-aleck imitation of their first meeting. "Cute. But no, actually I came to see your boss, and don't worry, I cleared it with Iris first. I'm waiting for him to get out of his meeting."

Unorganized thoughts ricocheted through her mind. She had so much to do before Saturday, but could she really just let Nathan corner Brad? Despite her employer's feeling that the Christmas party had gone well, she actually suspected that Nathan had left with an opinion lowered by Brad overselling himself and the company. Was Brad's meeting today with Mark, the company's lawyer? Maybe Mark's reminders of the gravity of the situation would make her boss more discreet.

One could always hope.

Whatever the case, she didn't want Nathan to know she was alarmed by his presence. He'd intimated that the story was a nonissue without any new leads. So why would he be here today unless he thought he had one?

With deliberate casualness, she turned to her computer screen. "Well, I'm sure he'll be with you shortly."

"Iris said about five minutes. She's a nice lady," he added, a bemused smile on his face. "I was on my cell phone outside when I called, and she kept fussing over whether or not I was warm enough out there."

Sheryl laughed. "That's Iris, all right. Affectionate grandmother to the whole staff." Brad's secretary clucked after him like a mother hen and treated everybody else the same way.

Suddenly straightening, Nathan squared his shoulders and shot her a cynical, assessing glance. "I guess you guys are just the biggest, happiest family of any corporation in Seattle, aren't you?"

"Excuse me?"

"Brad's the quintessential lovable big brother who just wants the best for all his employees and Iris is everyone's grandma." His tone suggested this was the most ridiculous theory ever put forth.

"You find it so impossible to believe that Brad might actually care about his staff?" She though it was a sad commentary on today's society that people who gave a damn about others were considered suspect.

"You said you don't read the *Sojourner*, but I assume you do get some news? That you aren't completely oblivious to the world we live in?" When she would have retorted, he held up a hand. "Look, I'm not some jaded guy who thinks there are no decent people left, but I'm not so gullible that I automatically trust people who are so nice they verge on saccharine, either."

Saccharine? Brad wasn't perfect, she'd be the first to say it—as long as she wasn't saying it to a journalist who might twist her words. But despite his flaws, Brad had heart. Maybe the concept of big-heartedness was more plausible to her because of the large, loving family she'd grown up in. Although even *she* was put off by a man so sensitive he went through an entire box of tissues after one *Titanic* viewing.

She wondered what Nathan's background had been like. Perhaps reporting others' misdeeds for long enough could eventually embitter a person, but it wasn't as though he were a grizzled old news veteran. Had something in his past predisposed him to believe the worst about people?

"I almost feel sorry for you." She hadn't meant to voice the fleeting thought, and she instantly regretted it.

Especially since he seemed to misinterpret genuine concern for pity meant to bait him. He narrowed his eyes, so dark they were almost black. "Save it for someone else. Like people who get conned easily and feel like suckers later. Or people whose ideas are stolen," he added pointedly.

"This again!" His mulish unwillingness to even consider that Brad might be telling the truth made her want to literally stomp her feet. "You're unbelievable! Did you come here just to pick a f—"

A low-pitched squeak of distress cut her off, and for the first time she noticed that Elliot had been approaching her office. He peeked tentatively around Nathan's broader frame. "Sorry to disturb you, Ms. Dayton. I just came up from the office downstairs to, um, finish our talk. But...some other time." He was already scuttling backward as he spoke.

She sighed. First he encountered her growling at coffeepots, now yelling at people in her office. Lovely. "I'm sorry, Elliot. If you want to stop by tomorrow and—"

"That's all right, Ms. Dayton, I know you're busy." His wide eyes regarded her as though he feared coming back tomorrow would only find her biting the heads off live chickens. "It wasn't that important anyway."

Trying to prove she was capable of normal, courteous behavior, she half rose from her chair, gesturing toward Nathan. "Did I get a chance at the Christmas party to introduce you to Nathan Hall? Nathan, this is Elliot Loomis, one of our most brilliant—"

"You're that reporter guy, aren't you? The one covering the..." If possible, Elliot's eyes had grown wider in his pale face. "I gotta go, Ms. Dayton. Sorry I bothered you both."

He disappeared from view quickly. His retreating footsteps were accompanied by a female's annoyed "Ow! Watch where you're going" that suggested Grace had finally returned from the printers. Apparently Elliot wasn't making progress on his mission to woo her.

Now more weary than angry, Sheryl turned back to Nathan. Truthfully, she wasn't sure how she'd let herself get provoked into such an uncontrolled response. Most of the heat had drained from his expression, as well. Whatever the reason he'd decided to wait for Brad in her office, it apparently hadn't been to pick a fight.

"I get that I'm not exactly Seattle's favorite son around here," he said, "but do I really bear that strong a resemblance to the bogeyman? The kid looked terrified."

She sat back down. "If it makes you feel any better, his horror was probably directed at me. I'm afraid he has the odd habit of catching me only when I'm making myself look bad."

His gaze softened, brushing over her in a very masculine appraisal. "You looking bad, there's a concept I can't wrap my mind around."

"I—I meant *behaving* badly."

"I doubt you do that often, either. Not intentionally, at any rate. You're just a very passionate woman."

Passionate. Most of her friends and family used words like temperamental and stubborn. No one had ever softly defended her from herself by telling her she was passionate in a velvet tone that slid over her like a verbal caress.

She was staring at him, but she couldn't make herself look away. It was as though she wanted to memorize his face, this unexpected moment. Ordinarily, she might have been embarrassed to be openly gawking, but since he was staring, too, she guessed it was all right.

Not just staring, she amended. Staring should be blank, motionless. Nathan's gaze was neither, trailing down over her features, pausing momentarily at her mouth before tracing a brief but unhurried path over her body that left a wake of warmth. She could almost feel individual cells...*buzzing* seemed the only word for it, right under her skin. Not quite ticklish, but definitely sensitive. Though the tingling sensation was far from painful, might even have been enjoyable under different circumstances, it was unsettling.

She breathed a quick sigh when he finished the seconds-long head-to-toe journey that had seemed to go on forever, but her relief floundered when he lifted his gaze back to her mouth. Passionate, he'd said. Followed by an admiring, speculative visual tour that left her skin heated.

Her lips parted slightly, and his eyes darkened even more.

"Nathan, my man!" Brad's hearty greeting made them both jump nearly a foot.

Well, Nathan jumped. Sheryl was still seated, but

she certainly *felt* as if she'd jumped. Or maybe just her heart had. It now seemed to be pounding in her throat rather than in its proper chest location.

"I was glad to get your call," Brad continued saying to their guest, oblivious to the sexual tension that hovered in her office like a dense blanket of low-lying clouds. "Sorry you had to wait for me to finish my teleconference."

"No problem."

Sheryl was impressed that Nathan managed to find his voice so quickly, but she noted his previously velvet tone now sounded as smooth and soft as shards of glass.

As the two men shook hands, Brad sent Sheryl a triumphant look that made her think of a cocker spaniel her family had once had. The dog would habitually bring them the nauseating but well-meaning gift of a dead animal, then wait proudly for his pat on the head. No doubt her employer thought Nathan's presence here was the natural progression of Brad's attempted bonding at the Christmas party and that the plan to show Nathan they were swell folks was en route to success.

Even if Nathan hadn't been in earshot, she wasn't sure how to break it to her boss that only minutes ago, the columnist had claimed Brad was "too nice" to possibly be genuine, then tossed out veiled accusations that reiterated his conviction of Brad's guilt.

"I'm going to show Nathan around the office," Brad said. "Let him see how everything works firsthand. Maybe take him out for one of those outrageously expensive business lunches."

"Oh, that won't be necessary," Nathan interrupted.

"At the very least, I can have Iris order us some

sandwiches," Brad said, his blue eyes still full of that puppyesque desire to please.

How could Nathan look at her boss and see a crook? Okay, she supposed that if you didn't know Brad, he could be a little much to take. On second thought, she knew Brad quite well and had dumped him because he *was* too much to take, but still...

Should I go with them?

Brad wore a goofy grin and had already called Nathan "my man." He'd proven with his relaxed attitude around the office that he didn't always proceed with the most professional behavior. If he thought Nathan had warmed up to him, he was likely to be twice as exuberant as normal. Nathan would probably see the potentially daunting flood of goodwill as insincerity.

But she hadn't been able to get Brad to dial it down a notch at the Christmas party, and if she noticeably intervened, she might seem as though she were trying to cover for Brad or make him look less guilty of something. Besides, this festival on Saturday wasn't going to run itself.

"Sandwiches sound good," Nathan conceded.

"Great! Sheryl, will you be joining us?"

"No. Thank you." She stared at her computer monitor as though it held the solution to the world's energy crisis instead of just her cartoon-pandas screen saver. "I have a ton of work to do."

Both men said goodbye to her, and she made a noncommittal noise but didn't dare glance up until they'd gone, feeling as drained as if she'd run a marathon. In a short span of time, she'd gone through shock to find Nathan in her doorway, unwise excitement to see him, amusement over their exchanged remarks, anger with his stubbornness and, finally, uncensored lust.

It would be nice to say that her own rational intelligence had put an end to the desire she'd felt as he'd practically seduced her with his eyes. But the truth was if Brad hadn't happened along when he did...

Well, she didn't know exactly. But the words *quickie* and *desk* whispered through her mind.

SHAKING HANDS with the latest software engineer Brad was introducing, Nathan thought to himself that he'd met one too many guys in the past few hours who wore glasses and spoke the native language C++. He could no longer tell them apart.

He and Brad had started upstairs once the promised sandwiches had arrived and had sat at a metallic sharp-edged desk that made Nathan's demonically possessed office chair look user-friendly. Over lunch, he'd made casual inquiries about what Brad thought his chances were if the case went to court. The other man reiterated that the attorneys were doing everything possible to reach a settlement without a trial—although from what Nathan knew about Kendra Mathers, she wanted her day in court. Brad had added that if it did go that far, of course they'd win; how could they lose, when they'd done nothing wrong?

Nathan hadn't bothered to respond to the flawed statement, knowing perfectly well from his dad's years as a cop that justice wasn't infallible. Either Brad was seriously naive or seriously fake, and since he ran a thriving software company and was touted to be a genius, Nathan had trouble buying the ingenuousness.

He'd followed up on Brad's confidence, pushing too hard. "So you'd go on record as stating your chances for a win are strong? There's nothing, say, in the way your company operates or in your past that might mislead a jury into thinking—"

"You know what, I really shouldn't be discussing this without my lawyer around," Brad had suddenly remembered. For the first time since Nathan had met him, the other man looked nervous. Then he'd hustled Nathan out of the office, abandoning their one-on-one conversation in favor of introducing Nathan to the programmers and designers who worked on the games.

In the infancy of Hammond Gaming Software, Brad explained, he'd overseen software design himself, but his job had become too big for that. While he approved all games before they went into development, designers did the grunt work. In this case, he claimed *Xandria Quest* was his idea, but he'd turned over the particulars to a team of programmers.

Nathan hadn't minded being rushed from Brad's upstairs office down to the sprawling, rectangular workspace filled with computer terminals and software enthusiasts, mostly men who all looked younger than he was. He'd hoped to pick up new leads from the people who'd worked on *Xandria Quest*.

Unfortunately, Nathan only understood every fifth word these programmers said. As the man in front of him launched into a proud, excited monologue about *Xandria Quest*'s use of nonrational quadratics, polygons and improvements on OpenGLs, Nathan blinked.

Make that every *sixth* word.

Clearing his throat, Nathan asked, "So Brad says you're the guy in charge. Were you the lead designer on *Xandria Quest*?"

The man shook his head, thankfully abandoning his rhapsody on how physics was making new games more realistic and involved. "No, *usually* I'm the guy in charge. I've been lead designer on most of our epic RPGs, but *Xandria* was Elliot's baby."

Brad smiled, his eyes losing their tense, guarded expression for the first time since Nathan had asked about his past. "Elliot Loomis, right over there." He pointed at a nearby cubicle.

Nathan glanced in the direction Brad was indicating, finding the same light-haired kid he'd met outside Sheryl's office. The younger man was hunched over an ergonomic keyboard, typing so fast Nathan expected to see sparks flying.

"One of my youngest designers, graduated college early," Brad said. "He might not have the same experience as some of my other great engineers, but he's a certified genius. A couple of the gaming magazines want to interview him."

"I'd like to interview him myself," Nathan replied, already moving in Elliot's direction. "So has he been the lead designer on any other games?"

"No, this was his big break. But he deserved it, and he was the right man for the job. When it came to this game and my vision for it, we...let's just say Elliot and I were on the same wavelength."

As they reached his desk, Elliot jerked his head up, looking flustered, dazed as though they'd disturbed him from deep thought. He glanced at Brad with something like nervous hero worship, but then his gaze slid to Nathan. Recognition clicked, and Nathan saw the same panicky expression that had been on the kid's face that morning.

Elliot shot out of his chair. "Hi, Mr. Hammond. Um, Mr. H-Hall."

Nathan offered a reassuring smile and firm but non-

threatening handshake. Elliot looked like a cub reporter who was over deadline and had just been cornered by his editor. This morning, Sheryl had claimed
the kid was afraid of *her*. She'd either assumed wrong
or had been covering. Clearly Nathan was the cause of
the kid's edginess.

"Elliot, you probably know I work for the *Sojourner*.
I wanted to talk to you about *Xandria Quest*, if you
don't mind."

"Not at all. But you caught me just as I was about to
take a break."

"We could talk upstairs then," Nathan offered,
"over coffee."

"Er...wrong kind of break." Elliot glanced at the
men's room in the nearby corner of the rectangular
workspace. "If you'll excuse me."

He dashed off for the rest room, and Nathan had a
hunch that if he tried to wait the kid out, he'd be sitting
here past sundown.

With a sigh, he glanced back at Brad. "I guess I'll just
talk to him some other time."

Brad nodded, his expression giving nothing away.
What did he think about his boy-wonder's hasty retreat? "You want to talk to the guys down here a little
more?"

And take notes on curvature and the future of poly-
counts? "That's okay. I think I'll head upstairs for that
coffee."

Brad escorted him as far as the elevator before remembering that he'd had a minor detail he wanted to
discuss with one of his team leaders.

Nathan stepped inside the parted doors, shaking his
head. The man who'd so desperately wanted to be his
buddy up until lunch was now avoiding conversation

with him, and *Xandria*'s lead designer fled every time he saw Nathan. *And I'm supposed to believe there's no story here?*

Right. Almost as believable as his telling himself he hadn't been one bad decision away from kissing Sheryl in her office.

9

FOR THE DURATION of the afternoon, once she'd finally gotten all her mental synapses firing again, Sheryl multitasked like crazy. Her job deserved her full attention. And maybe if she worked hard enough, she wouldn't dwell on Nathan Hall and the electricity she felt between them earlier.

And maybe Santa Claus really did exist and would leave her a few pairs of Jimmy Choos for being such a good girl this year.

Still, at least she'd accomplished a lot. In fact, at almost four, she realized she'd not only tunneled through what she'd wanted to finish today, but made a head start on her projects for tomorrow. With an alarmed double take at the clock in the corner of her computer screen, she chastised herself for not calling Meka back by now. No doubt her roommate was proceeding with dinner as planned.

She grabbed the phone and dialed Meka's work number. Voice mail. Knowing her friend's flexible schedule and hours spent at customer locations, Sheryl tried the cell phone number but got voice mail again. *No, thank you.* A missed message would lead to Sheryl having dinner with Dane tonight.

Now that she'd finally come up for air, might as well take a break. She stood, deciding to grab a cup of coffee before trying Meka again.

"Grace?" Sheryl pushed open her office door, looking around to see if she should bring back a cup for her assistant, or maybe something from the vending machine.

But the other woman wasn't at her desk. Sheryl rolled her eyes. The approaching holidays must have temporarily crimped Grace's work ethic. First, she'd taken about three times longer than expected at the printers, then she'd extended her lunch by an unapproved forty-five minutes because she'd apparently lost track of time listening to carolers at the mall's food court.

Never mind. Sheryl had probably done enough work for both of them today, and she could overlook an occasional lapse in a normally reliable employee.

But her feelings of benevolence didn't survive discovering Grace standing at the breakroom counter with Nathan Hall, giggling at something he'd just said.

What is he still doing here?

Sheryl hadn't seen Brad since he'd left her office earlier, but she'd assumed the two men had parted ways hours ago. "Well, hello. I didn't expect to find you here."

Grace started, obviously thinking Sheryl meant her. "I was going to tell you I was taking a quick break, but you seemed like you were on such a roll this afternoon, I didn't want to bother you."

"You know you don't have to check with me to take your break," Sheryl felt obligated to answer.

Of course, how much of a break the young woman could possibly need after being gone practically all day was another story. But Sheryl resisted the urge to say anything shrewish.

Especially since she doubted her motivation to do so

was work-related. All she could think about was Grace's quasi-mystical ability to pick up hunks. Nathan certainly qualified for hunk-status, and Grace's body language indicated she'd noticed. Then again, what woman with working eyesight and a pulse wouldn't?

"Really, I was just headed back to work," Grace blurted, stepping away from her cozy position alongside Nathan. "I was even bringing you a mug of coffee." She lifted two mugs from the counter, holding one toward Sheryl.

"Thanks." Sheryl bit back a sigh. "Tell you what, instead of trying to get back in the groove of things this close to five, why not just knock off early?"

"Honestly?"

"Sure."

Her assistant headed for the door, not waiting to be told twice. "See you in the morning, then. Nice running into you again, Mr. Hall!"

"That was nice of you," Nathan commented wryly once they were alone.

Please don't let him guess that I latched on to a reason to get rid of her because I was—she wouldn't allow herself to think of the word *jealous*, but it hovered just below conscious thought. Like something unseen to the naked eye but that smelled bad just the same.

"I'm a nice person." You could be nice *and* envious of your size four, not-as-close-to-thirty assistant at the same time, right? "I keep telling you we exist, but you're determined to find deviousness and corruption."

He scowled. "The only thing I'm trying to find is the truth."

"By hanging out in the breakroom flirting with a

young female employee? Or is that how you usually get information for your columns?" she heard herself challenge, knowing she was overreacting but unable to catch herself before giving in to the irritated impulse.

"You make it sound like I was in the nefarious act of seducing a minor." He snorted, and though she already knew her accusation was silly, she found herself glad he was about to deny it. "She's definitely old enough to be a consenting adult."

Ack! That hadn't been what he was supposed to say. "You're old enough to be her..." Slightly older brother?

Deflated, she told herself to let it go before she wound up looking even more idiotic than she already did.

Nathan smirked. "Is there a particular reason you're trying to suddenly paint me as a member of the AARP?"

"Well," she attempted weakly, "if you *were* a retired person, you wouldn't be writing about Hammond anymore."

He took a couple of steps toward her, and her heart hammered in her ears. She experienced that tension that had been in her office all over again, only this time there was no furniture between them.

There's never a faux-cherrywood desk around when you need one.

"I don't think your comments had anything to do with retirement," Nathan countered. "I think they stemmed from jealousy."

"Jealousy!" She wanted to tell him to get over himself, that he could flirt with every female from here to Tacoma, that she had no interest in him whatsoever, had barely noticed he was even male.

Of course, lightning would strike her dead on the spot, so she simply repeated her indignant, if not particularly witty, "Jealousy!" Since he looked more amused than put in his place by her outrage, she managed to tack on, "That makes no sense."

"No more sense than wanting to stab Brad with my chopsticks every time he touched your hand at the Christmas party."

Melting at record-breaking speed, she felt as disoriented as an iceberg suddenly finding itself in the Bahamas. "Really?"

"*Is* there something between the two of you?"

She swallowed. "You asking for investigative purposes?"

"No." His gaze locked with hers.

"We dated at one time. For a little while. Nothing serious. We're just friends."

He nodded, his expression neutral, his silent acceptance of her explanation indicating the subject was closed. But his dark eyes seemed to ask, is there something between the two of *us?*

Simply because she so badly wanted to take a step *closer* to him, she shuffled back. If he tried to kiss her, she'd end up the subject of tawdry office gossip—the public relations manager who had personal relations up against the soda machine. And if he didn't try to kiss her, well, she might try to kiss him. The result would either be rejection—shudder—or aforementioned soda machine scandal.

What she needed to do was get away. Now. Maybe do as she'd suggested to Grace and go home early. Home—her thoughts barreled into one another like a freeway pile-up. The apartment, her roommate, a dinner date Sheryl still hadn't managed to cancel beyond a shadow of a doubt.

"I have a phone call to make," she recalled abruptly.

She pivoted on her heel, but Nathan lightly gripped her elbow. "Wait. Sheryl, you aren't really angry about Grace, are you?"

She looked over her shoulder, falling into the hypnotic pull of his nearness, his touch, the scent of his warm, spicy cologne. "No."

"Good." His eyes strayed to his hand on her arm, as though he were willing himself to let go of her. But he merely relaxed his hold. "Because you do know, I hope, that I don't hit on women to get information...and she wouldn't have been the one I hit on anyway. Hypothetically speaking," he added, even though there was nothing hypothetical about the way he was looking at her.

Heat flooded her face, and she told herself it was completely inappropriate to hope he'd try to seduce her into betraying her boss. "Hypothetically, if you were to try to sweet-talk me out of information, all you'd get for your trouble would be scathing glares and biting condemnation."

"Your scathing glares are growing on me," he told her, his gruff voice oddly affectionate. "So...wanna have dinner with me this evening and let me try to sweet-talk you?"

"What?"

He held his hands up in front of him. "I know, I know. It will only result in your scorching disapproval, but apparently I'm a sucker for abuse."

Sheryl cocked her head to the side. He seemed to be speaking in clear English, and she did have a college degree. Yet her brain couldn't process his words. "Did you just invite me to dinner?"

Though his expression was slightly bemused, he widened his smile. "Sounded like it, didn't it?"

Well, she was going to say no, of course. How completely out of her mind would she have to be to say anything else?

It gives you a great excuse to tell Meka under no uncertain terms that you won't be there for dinner, a small voice chirped.

She knew that voice—it was the one that always popped up to rationalize bad decisions. The devil on her shoulder, she imagined. Apparently, the angelic counterpart was locked away in a trunk somewhere.

The rationalizations continued. She'd proven that spending time with other men wasn't the way to exorcise Nathan from her thoughts. Maybe this tension between them was mere curiosity, mystery, the allure of what-if. Perhaps she could get him out of her system if they spent a little time together.

Before common sense could reassert itself, she nodded. "Dinner sounds good. Just let me make a quick phone call, and you think about where we should meet." That way, instead of his bringing her back here for her car afterwards, she could get straight home. All the quicker to check herself into some twelve-step program for women who make unwise romantic decisions.

Not necessarily unwise, the devil on her shoulder insisted. Maybe dinner tonight with Nathan could be excused with the same principle she always used when dieting—have some extra chocolate before the day she started to get her cravings out of the way.

Given how much she'd wanted to taste him only seconds ago, the comparison to chocolate was alarmingly appropriate.

"You in the mood for anything in particular?" Nathan asked.

"Wh-whatever restaurant you like is fine," she was relieved to hear herself say. Because "You and a bottle of chocolate syrup" might have been inappropriate. Not to mention the mess it would've made of her bedsheets.

10

NATHAN SETTLED into a spindle-backed chair, glancing around the interior of the familiar restaurant as though seeing it for the first time. The cozy atmosphere created by small round tables and dark, rustic wood-paneling seemed overly intimate tonight. Or maybe that was only because his nerves were so sensitized by Sheryl's nearness. By her smile, by the perfume he'd noticed during their walk from the parking garage, despite the wind that should have chased it away.

He didn't know which surprised him more, that she'd agreed to go out with him, or that he'd asked. He certainly hadn't had any plans to do so, not after this afternoon's events had convinced him that Brad was definitely hiding something. And that Elliot Loomis might be part of it, too.

Then again, even if there were a small conspiracy at Hammond Gaming Software, Sheryl wasn't necessarily part of it. She was so candid in her emotions that it was hard to believe her guilty of deception.

Or was that just his attraction to her talking?

She leaned back in her own chair, scanning the menu she'd opened. Delicate tendrils of hair had slipped free of her braid some time during the day, framing her face and softening her already too-inviting appearance. "So, what's good here?"

He lifted an eyebrow. "You actually want me to

make recommendations?'' She glanced up at his tone, prompting him to quickly add, ''That wasn't meant to be sarcastic, honest. You just seem like someone who likes to make her own decisions.''

Her fathomless eyes held his for another second, and he doubted he'd feel any more scorched if he stuck his finger into the flame of the tear-drop-shaped candle burning between them on the center of the table. She nodded, apparently convinced of his nonsarcastic intentions.

''I do like to make my own decisions,'' she said. ''But I'm not opposed to advice from others before I make one. The thing I always hated was when men tried to order for me, especially without consulting me first! Brad used to—'' She broke off, her teeth sinking into the fullness of her lower lip.

Nathan wondered what it said about his mental state that he was jealous of teeth.

''I really shouldn't have brought him up,'' she said apologetically. ''In fact, this evening will probably go better if neither one of us does.''

Though her perfectly logical statement was said in a light, contemplative tone, he knew he'd just been warned. Fine by him. He didn't want to fight over her boss or her company. He wasn't even a reporter tonight, just a man.

Still, to see her smile, he teased her, ''So much for my nefarious plans to sweet-talk you, then.''

She did grin, as he'd hoped, but only for a second. ''I know that's not why you asked me out, you have more integrity than that. So, what *did* make you decide to—''

''You folks know what you'd like to drink this evening?'' A young man in a denim shirt and khaki slacks stood at Nathan's elbow, his pencil poised to take down beverage and appetizer orders.

Nathan had never been so happy to see a waiter in his entire life.

"YOU DID NOT," Sheryl protested laughingly. Though Nathan was right about the excellent food here, she kept getting too engrossed in their conversation to remember to eat. She'd laughed so hard tonight her face hurt.

"I did. What can I say?" His eyes twinkled in the candlelight, and she sensed he deliberately wasn't finishing his story to keep her hanging on his every word. She could have told him the dramatic pause wasn't necessary.

Though there had been a couple of awkward conversational moments earlier, Nathan had enough journalistic experience to ask questions without making her feel as though she was being interrogated. An only child himself, he'd seemed highly entertained by her big family anecdotes, and he'd returned the favor by regaling her with adventures from his one "misbegotten semester" in college. The time he'd spent with his mischievous roommate had been a sharp contrast to the stern picture Nathan painted of life with his dad, and Sheryl got the impression Nathan had needed a little rebellion.

Sheryl was currently laughing over Nathan's disastrous Spring Break trip to Florida with the roommate and another buddy. The less than auspicious beginning to their road trip had been a freeway breakdown, followed by the hotel from hell, since they were scrimping in order to have more beer money. He'd explained how his friends had dared him to go skinny-dipping at a crowded public beach to impress some slightly older women who were sunbathing.

"Well," she demanded, "did you impress them?"

She'd been so caught up in the hilarity of his descriptions that she hadn't been in the right frame of mind to picture him naked in the surf. But now, as she stopped long enough to dwell on it, she suspected Nathan Hall in all his glory would be an impressive sight indeed. Suddenly dry-mouthed, she grasped the water glass in front of her.

He shook his head. "Actually, I don't think they were wowed by my shout of surprise and pain... No sooner had I dropped my trunks and jumped in the water than I got stung on the butt by a jellyfish."

Sheryl choked on her water. "Seriously?"

"Scout's honor."

"You were a scout?"

"Not really," he admitted. "That would have been hard on Dad, getting me to meetings and taking me camping and all the stuff that comes with it."

She wanted to reach across the table and take his hand. He'd barely mentioned his mother, but each time he did, a note of unresolved pain crept into his voice. It must be doubly hard now that his father had passed away, too.

"How did your mom die?" Sheryl asked softly, wondering if it would help him to talk about it.

He drew back in his chair, eyes wide, appearing startled by the question. "She's not dead. She lives in Phoenix."

"What?" When he'd first mentioned her... Sheryl couldn't recall what his exact wording had been, but his manner had been so *final*. He'd made it clear that his mother was irrevocably gone from his life, leaving

Sheryl with the obviously mistaken impression that his mother had died when he was young. "So your parents were just divorced, then?"

He pushed away the rest of his seafood linguini. "She went to the grocery store one day and never came back."

"Oh. Nathan, I'm so—"

"Don't."

They both flinched at his sharp tone, and he lowered his voice, an apology flickering in his eyes. "I think I turned out better with just Dad as a role model. He was busting his butt trying to protect and serve, and all she could do was complain about how hard it was being a cop's wife. When the scandal in his precinct broke…"

After a long minute of staring off into space, he met Sheryl's gaze. "You don't really want to hear my sob story."

Actually, she did. She'd been enjoying his entertaining anecdotes, but she was more interested in the pain that pinched at his mouth and darkened his eyes. She sensed that if she really wanted to know him, she needed to understand this part of his life.

And just when had she decided it was so important to truly know Nathan Hall?

Choosing her words carefully, she said, "I don't want to make you uncomfortable by talking about it, but—"

"Not at all." He shrugged with such forced casualness that she hurt for him. "She doesn't bother me. Dad made me see that we were better off without her."

Picking up the thread of his prematurely halted story, Nathan explained how his father had discovered some other cops in the precinct were on the take and wanted to turn them in to Internal Affairs. His mother had opposed the idea, not wanting her husband to make waves when he was up for a promotion. But Nathan's dad had followed his sense of integrity, and the resulting strain, both in the precinct and at home, had ended the marriage.

"And you don't talk to her?" Sheryl couldn't imagine life without her family, though, Heaven knew she'd tried often enough.

"What would I say? Dad raised me to live life the way he did, in black-and-white. With ethical standards." He flashed a weak smile. "And with the exception of a few misspent months in college, I've tried to stick by that... She never understood him, and she wouldn't understand me, either."

Well. Sheryl certainly wouldn't have to worry about the ache in her cheeks from laughing anymore.

The ache in her heart was something else entirely. Though Nathan spoke of his dad with great respect, she noticed that his memories were more about the man's integrity and job responsibilities than affection toward his son.

Sheryl—beleaguered by a brother she had covered for when he got into messes and sisters who had the audacity to call her round the clock for romantic advice even while criticizing her comparative lack of boyfriends—had often thought she'd like more solitude. But looking at Nathan, who was completely alone... well, she couldn't say she envied him.

Was the bitter cynicism that sometimes tinted his voice and expression strictly his, or a legacy inherited after years spent with a disapproving father still angry with his ex-wife?

Oh, brother. Catching herself in the midst of unasked for, uneducated pop-psychology, she did a mental eye

roll. Nathan was ticked at his mom and had every right
to be. It was none of Sheryl's business. Certainly no
reason for her to turn all broody, filled with the sudden
impulse to offer to kiss him and make it all better. But
her original innocent intentions must have taken a
wrong turn somewhere because the steamy images of
shared kisses that flashed through her mind had very
little to do with comforting. And everything to do with
trying to remember where her diaphragm was.

"Sheryl?"

"Y-yes?"

"Thought I'd lost you for a minute."

No. You had me for a minute.

"Sorry, all this talk about family got me thinking
about mine." Sensing he wouldn't appreciate the rev-
elation that his own upbringing made her suddenly
appreciate hers, she tacked on lamely, "I'm supposed
to see them this weekend and then again on Christmas,
and I still have a ton of shopping to do."

He signaled the waiter for the check. "You want to
walk off some of this meal? There are some great stores
in the area, and we could window-shop at FAO
Schwarz." His eyes lit up when he mentioned the re-
nowned toy store. "I can't wait until Kaylee and Frank
have kids so I can spoil them rotten."

A smile tugged at her mouth. Despite the occasional,
cynical barrier he erected, Nathan did have a softer
side.

"Sure," she agreed, not quite ready to end the evening. She reached for her scarf and mittens. "That
sounds nice."

Nice? What an insipid word for strolling through the
crisp cold, huddled close to share warmth beneath
stars and Christmas lights, with the man who'd so ef-

fortlessly captured her attention and focus. And seemed, with each passing second, more capable of capturing her heart.

NATHAN STOOD next to Sheryl, both of them acting like bedazzled children with their noses practically pressed against the glass. Except his thoughts about his lovely, empathetic companion with curves not even her overcoat could completely obscure, were purely the adult kind.

Their breath came out in white, foggy bursts, mingling as they discussed their favorite selections inside.

"I just don't see you as the doll type," he said, amused by her retroactive coveting of the pink three-story dream home displayed. "Dolls seem so...girly."

She raised her eyebrows. "And were you under the impression that I grew up a little boy?"

Definitely not. Sheryl was all woman.

Her gaze locked on to something, and she pointed toward a doll with a halo of blond curls, costumed in iridescent pale blue and silver.

"Isn't she beautiful?" Sheryl breathed.

The porcelain figure had nothing on Sheryl's bright eyes and cheeks rosy with the cold, but he nodded politely.

"I always wanted a doll like that," she continued, "but they're for decoration only. I didn't have my own room, so there wasn't a lot of space for what my mom called 'dust magnets,' and I was always afraid my brother might mess one up, anyway. He was a good guy, but always roughhousing. I—'' She glanced sidelong in Nathan's direction and broke off when she noticed his gaze.

He shifted his weight, feeling almost guilty. Was it

wrong to lust after a woman caught up in the past in-nocence of her childhood? Probably.

"I'm not sure what the big deal is," he blustered. "Even with the dolls you *did* get to play with. So you change their clothes and brush their hair. It's not like they save the world from the forces of evil." His gaze fell on a fatigue-clad action figure that came with much cooler weaponry than any he'd ever had growing up.

"Aha!" Sheryl smirked. "So you played with dolls, too."

"*Soldiers*, Ms. Dayton. Not dolls. Clearly you don't understand the difference."

She laughed, appraising the plastic action figure in the window. "I understand that he's the right size to fit in one of the tuxedoes or tennis outfits of my old Ke—"

"Blasphemy! Don't you dare finish that sentence. *He*," Nathan clarified, gesturing inside, "is a man of ac-tion, not a yuppie playboy."

"Well, if it makes you feel better, I like action, too." Her pink cheeks darkened even further, and she stared straight ahead. "I mean, my dolls were superspies. In-stead of just sitting around their sadly inferior one-story dream home, they worked to save the world from the forces of evil just like yours did. But my dolls had really kick-ass matching accessories to do it with."

Nathan chuckled. "Okay, that does sound more like you."

Laughing with him, Sheryl turned, resting her head sideways against the glass, so close he could almost feel the softness of her face against his.

As their gazes met again, the laughter between them faded. Did she have any idea how beautiful she was? Or how much he wanted to kiss her right now?

Almost as if she knew exactly that, she stiffened and stepped away from the glass abruptly.

"Thanks again for the...for dinner," she said.

Dinner. Not necessarily a date.

Because those ended in kisses, didn't they?

She laid a hand on her purse strap. "You sure you don't want me to pay you for my half?"

Gee, could she make it any more obvious that tonight hadn't been a date? Still, why should that annoy him? Sheryl Dayton was a complication he didn't need in his life. He should be glad that at least one of them was thinking clearly.

He tore his gaze from her face and glanced once more in the store window. A toy train jogged around an elaborate track, flashing red sirens that Nathan didn't have to hear through the thick glass to understand.

"Come on," he offered. "I'll walk you back to your car."

When she nodded, they turned in the direction of the parking garage. He was distantly aware that the night held a damp chill, but it barely touched him with Sheryl by his side. Heat thrummed through him, along with the urge to hold her against him. Would she pull away, or snuggle closer?

They reached the shelter of the parking garage, stepping under the otherworldly wash of pale orange overhead lights. He escorted Sheryl to her car, the only sound between them their footsteps on the concrete.

She stuck her key in the lock, then paused. "I had a good time."

"Me, too."

Obviously about to say something else, she nervously moistened her lips with the tip of her tongue.

.An action that drew his attention to her too-kissable mouth. An action that eroded the self-control he'd been trying to convince himself he had.

He reached out and cupped her shoulders, pulling her closer even as he leaned toward her. His lips met hers in a soft explosion, two people meshing in an exploration more eager than gentle. He swept his tongue across the seam of her lips, teasing and coaxing, groaning when she rubbed her tongue against his. The sound was absorbed by their kiss.

Slowly stepping forward, maneuvering Sheryl backward, he brought them to rest against the side of her car. Threading his fingers in her hair, he angled his head to deepen the kiss. Even though he knew he was already in far too deep and over his head.

Sheryl's slow, approving murmur was music to his ears, but too quickly, the approving sound became a sigh and she turned her head to the side.

"Wait, Nathan. I—this is exactly like the soda machine, only against the car, and I didn't want to...well I *did* want to, but don't you think—"

Bereft of her kiss, he tried to round up what functioning brain cells he had left and concentrate on what she was saying. Unfortunately, the three surviving cells couldn't make any sense of her soda machine reference. "What's wrong?"

She gestured impatiently with her hands, sweeping them in front of her. "This. You. Me. Brad..."

Nathan's jaw tightened. What the hell was she doing thinking about *him* right now? "I thought we weren't going to mention that tonight."

"Trust me, I'd rather not. But don't you think we should, if we're going to..." Another vague, all-encompassing gesture.

"I see. If I'm going to kiss you, then you need some assurance that I'm not going to write about your company, is that it?"

"Of course not!" She looked genuinely startled by his conclusion, but he couldn't help but wonder why it was she had been thinking about their opposing work situations when all he'd been thinking about was the taste or her.

"Sheryl, this was a mistake."

"You don't say." Her sarcastic tone matched the anger that was slowly replacing the surprise in her expression. "Trust me, I never would have kissed you if I'd known you thought it was some sort of *office strategy*. Come to think of it, I didn't kiss you."

As she reminded him that he'd been the one who instigated their kiss, she climbed in her car, then slammed the door and revved the engine almost simultaneously. He might have been justified in pointing out that she'd kissed him back enthusiastically enough, but he was too busy getting out of the way. Her manner indicated that she was getting out of there now, and he suspected if she ran over his foot in the process, she'd consider that a bonus.

"Pizza delivery," Nathan announced Friday evening when Kaylee opened the door to the ranch-style Renton-suburb home.

"Oh, good. Frank, the food's arrived," she called over her shoulder.

Nathan smiled wryly. "I thought I was a treasured friend, turns out I'm just a quick way for the food to get here."

Her husband—a behemoth of a man dressed in a

gray S.P.D. sweatshirt and jeans—appeared in the foyer behind her.

"Good timing." Frank waved his free hand toward Nathan, clutching paper plates in the other. "I thought you were gonna miss tip-off."

"Not a chance." Nathan passed Kaylee the warm cardboard box that smelled like an oregano-seasoned slice of heaven and stepped inside the house, shrugging out of his jacket. "I've been looking forward to this game all week."

Yep, his week had been divided between work and looking forward to his standing basketball date at the Carpenters'. And kicking himself over the way he'd behaved with Sheryl Monday night, although he hadn't decided yet what he'd do differently if he could go back in time—not kiss her at all, the wise choice, or seduce her back into the kiss after she broke it off, the more tempting choice. Either move would have been better than accusing her of being some sort of public relations Mata Hari.

That's enough, he told himself sternly. He could maybe understand how a guy got preoccupied with unwanted thoughts while he was alone in his apartment, but he was among friends tonight and the game was about to start. He wasn't going to spend the evening remembering the way her eyes sparkled mischievously when she'd told that story about deliberately locking her brother's window after he snuck out. Or recalling the floral scent that had made outdoor Seattle in December seem like spring as she'd stood there making teasing allegations about Nathan once playing with dolls.

"Nathan?" Frank's puzzled tone made Nathan suddenly aware that he was now alone in the foyer. His hosts had rummaged through the kitchen and were en route to the den. "You staying, or just dropping off the pizza?"

"Sorry, my mind wandered for a minute. Lead on. I could use a cold beer and a couple of slices."

Two steps ahead of the men, Kaylee already had napkins and a six-pack of chilled bottles in her hand. "Pizza's on the coffee table. C'mon, the game's starting."

Nathan followed the sounds of the exuberant announcer and televised crowd and took his usual seat in the recently remodeled den. He'd spent last summer helping Frank repaint three of the walls and rebuild the faltering stone wall that housed the fireplace. The project had finally sealed the men's friendship. Up until then, Frank had been a little dubious about his undeniably gorgeous wife spending so much time with another man. Given divorce rates and Nathan's own experiences with people's often dishonest natures, Nathan had never blamed the man for his unvoiced suspicions.

Now, though, as Nathan glanced at the couple cuddled together on the sofa, he suspected there would never be a rival for Kaylee's affections. An oddly optimistic sentiment for a man who knew all the current statistics about failed relationships and cynically accepted them. It wasn't as though his own upbringing had given him high hopes for lasting marriage and happy ever afters. He was in the business of news, not fairy tales.

Kaylee turned her head, and he quickly redirected his gaze to the television, not quite focusing on the pass the Sonics' forward made to the center.

"Are you okay tonight?" she asked.

"I got beer, basketball and pizza. Why wouldn't I be okay?"

"Maybe because there's more to life than beer, basketball and pizza," she suggested softly, drawing surprised looks from both men.

"Honey," Frank chided, "guys aren't into all that sharing like you women."

"Guy or not, he's my friend. Besides," she added, lifting the remote and hitting the mute button, "they're going to commercial."

Frank pondered this, then nodded. Obviously, prying into Nathan's life held more entertainment potential than a department store ad for a new collection of designer towels.

Nathan took a swig from the bottle in his hands—the determined gleam in Kaylee's almond eyes warned he was going to need it.

"We love having you here," she said, "but don't you think it's kind of pathetic that we're your only life outside the office?"

"Kay!" Frank looked appalled. "He's not pathetic."

"No, of course not." Kaylee had the nerve to look stunned, as though she hadn't just suggested Nathan was. "He's smart, witty, good-looking... But Nathan, you push people away. Is this really the life you want?"

Leave it to Kaylee to make it sound as though something were tragically wrong with his life. He was well respected in his career and had dependable friends. At least, he normally considered Kaylee a friend, when she wasn't predicting a bleak, lonely future for him.

"You've got a real optimistic outlook," he teased. "Ever thought about being one of those nuts who walks around downtown with a The End is Near sign?"

"Don't joke." She frowned. "I'm trying to help you. You commented to me once that Frank and I are lucky to have each other, and I couldn't agree more, but you don't give yourself a chance at that same luck."

He felt his jaw clench. Didn't she know that what she and Frank shared was rare and nearly impossible to find? "I date."

"Not much," Frank cut in, putting to rest the myth of guys sticking together. "At first, I thought you had the hots for Kaylee, but then when I realized you didn't and you rarely had a girlfriend for more than two weeks, I thought for sure you were..." His sentence crumbled under the combined weight of Kaylee's and Nathan's glares.

"Going on occasional dates," Kaylee protested to Nathan, "is not the same as actual dating. You either walk out before she can, or chase her off by always looking for the worst in people."

Frank nodded suddenly, his face lit up at the prospect of contributing something that didn't involve Nathan's sexual orientation. "She's right! Remember that woman you met while you were researching the article on Pike's Place vendors? You went out with her a few times, but became convinced she was secretly married."

Kaylee groaned. "Bad example, dear. She did turn out to be married."

"You see?" Nathan held his hands palms up. "It's not that I think people are dishonest because I'm cynical. It's that I'm cynical because of all my experience with dishonest people. Frank, you see crooks and violence every day, you tell her." Nathan's world view had been shaped early on, even before his mother walked out, by his dad's stories of the type of men he was trying to protect the community from.

"Sorry." The big man shook his head, his gaze apologetic. "It's not that I don't see your point, man, but Kaylee's right. You can't just go around expecting the worst. Sure, I deal with thugs, but I run into a lot of good people. Witnesses who come forward even if it might mean danger for them, people who bring us lost wallets or purses and don't steal all the money or credit cards."

Nathan fought the urge to go bang his head against the fireplace. Since when had Frank become such a verbose advocate of seeing the world through rose-colored glasses?

Frank reached for the remote. "Game's back on."

The seemingly interminable commercial break from hell ended, but Nathan's relief was short-lived. As the first quarter passed in a blur, Kaylee's observations continued to plague him. When he'd kissed Sheryl, had he reached for an excuse to push her away afterward?

No, Kaylee's wrong. For one thing, Nathan hadn't even been the one to end the kiss. Besides, to paraphrase a well-known motto, just because he was paranoid didn't mean Brad Hammond wasn't crooked.

Still...was guilt on Brad's part automatically synonymous with subterfuge on Sheryl's? Recalling the shock on her face when he'd snapped at her, Nathan suspected he owed her an apology. He groaned inwardly. Saying he was sorry was not on his list of fun pastimes; then again, it gave him an excuse to see her again.

The HGS Holiday Festival Sheryl had so excitedly

discussed over dinner was tomorrow, the perfect opportunity for Nathan to talk to her. While he was at it, he could prove Kaylee wrong. He was just as capable of being in a holly jolly mood as anyone else in Seattle. Memories of past relationships—exceedingly *short* relationships—tried to surface, but he pushed them back under before he could analyze just what he'd done to drive other women away.

Although it was difficult to get ahold of some people and ask questions this close to the holidays, Beth the intern had been rechecking Hammond's background. She hadn't discovered anything Nathan didn't already know, certainly nothing that would confirm the hints that his mystery caller had given—that there was a dark secret lurking in Brad's past. Maybe Nathan should have taken the caller more seriously, but there wasn't much he could do with an anonymous woman who may or may not be a crackpot when there seemed to be no proof of her allegations. Conversely, if, by some miracle, Beth turned up a reason to exonerate Hammond, Nathan would graciously be the first to proclaim the man's innocence. They'd never be buddies, of course—jumping from the Space Needle was preferable to prolonged exposure to the other's man ceaseless cheer—but Nathan could admit when he was wrong.

Meanwhile, he was willing to admit that he'd probably been wrong about Sheryl's motivations in the parking garage. He'd show up at that festival tomorrow and be completely charming. Not a hint of cynicism in sight. Even if he caught Brad Hammond ripping off ideas from local teenagers who had entered Hammond's Game of the Future contest.

11

IT WAS ONLY 9:00 a.m., but already Sheryl had deduced that she should have stayed in bed this morning. Or she should at least escape back home before people began arriving at ten.

Speaking through clenched teeth, she asked the vendor, "What do you mean, no hot dogs?"

The wiry man in the wool cap and windbreaker shrugged. "I told you, my cart happened to be near the freeway last night when that eighteen-wheeler blocked all the lanes. People were there for hours, I sold out. I didn't have a chance to get any more before now."

"Not that I don't sympathize with the hungry people in the traffic jam, but you *knew* I'd booked you for this morning."

"Sure, but you can't tell me how much I would've sold. *This* was only prospective money on hot dog sales. Last night was guaranteed money." His beady eyes took on a sage gleam. "A wise man never turns down a sure opportunity handed to him by fate in favor of the unrealized possible opportunity yet to come."

Of all the hot dog vendors in the world, and she got the aspiring fortune-cookie writer.

"I still got buns," he told her. "And condiments. It could be like, um..." He snapped his fingers. "People buy them vegetarian burgers. This'll be like vegetarian hot dogs."

She pinched the bridge of her nose. "Vegetarian burgers have actual, specially made meatless patties. They aren't just ketchup and mustard on a bun."

"Meatless patties." He shuddered. "If you ask me, I'd rather just eat the bread than one of those soy-veggie things."

She hadn't asked him, but skipped pointing that out in favor of finding a solution. "Is there some reason you can't take care of the little supply problem now?"

"Out of the question. My regular supplier—"

"Couldn't you run to a grocery store or something?"

He scowled. "Lady, I get a nice wholesale discount. You want me to stock up at the local food mart, there's not going to be any profit for me. Are you planning to spring extra for the dogs?"

"I'm trying to raise money for charity!"

"Well, then I hope I sell a lot of buns you can profit from."

"You're honestly going to stay and sell bread?"

"You got someone else who needs my space?" When she shook her head, he added, "I can sell drinks to people."

Oh, good. When the angry mob cornered her, at least no one would be thirsty.

He ambled across the pavement back to his stand. On weekdays, the spacious parking lot of the business complex was filled with sedans and SUVs, but today's festival had redecorated the area with makeshift shelters. Booths run by HGS and its partner sponsors, tents set up by merchants who had rented space to sell arts and crafts and even a few carnival rides dotted the paved landscape. Sheryl shot a forlorn glance at the hot

dog stand, which was topped with a giant replica of a
frankfurter. Talk about false advertising. Looking toward a nearby cart fashioned to resemble a colorful
sombrero, she said a quick prayer that festival-goers
were in a taco-buying mood today.

The weenie man was the third person today to mess
up her plans. The first two had been the gangly teenage
boy she'd hired to be Santa's helper and the female
rent-an-elf who was supposed to take pictures. Apparently, love had bloomed fleetingly in the North Pole,
then withered and died in the harsh climate. From
what Sheryl had gathered during the nasty elf alterca-
tion this morning, the young lovers had broken up last
night. After exchanging a few choice words that would
have Santa leaving them both coal, they'd claimed they
couldn't be anywhere near each other, then both
stomped off the premises.

Not that the lack of elves was anything compared to
the unfortunate portable toilet situation. If someone
with plumbing solutions didn't call her back on her cell
phone soon, she wouldn't be held responsible for her
actions.

"Sheryl?"

"*What?*" She pivoted, already fixing a glare on the
hapless speaker. She'd let the hot dog guy off relatively
easy since she couldn't quite blame him for feeding a
hungry crowd, and the heartbroken elves hadn't stuck
around long enough for her lecture on contractual ob-
ligations. But woe to the next person who let her down.

Elliot leaped back, literally trembling in his—what
were those, regulation Star-Fleet-issue boots?

With a forced smile, she amended in a less off-with-
their-heads tone, "What can I do for you, Elliot?"

"Nothing," he said quickly. "Um, not a thing. Really. I just...this clearly isn't a good time."

He scampered back to the HGS booth where visitors would later be able to play free demos of next year's slotted releases. She supposed she'd officially lost Elliot's vote when it came time to nominate the company's employee of the year.

A hand tapped her shoulder.

This time she carefully pasted a wide smile on her face and tried to wipe any homicidal tendencies from her expression before turning. "Yes, can I h— Hi." After their meeting last week, she certainly hadn't expected to see Nathan today.

"Hi." His eyes locked with hers, and the electric current between them could no doubt power all the rented rides and space heaters even if the generators blew. Which, considering her luck, they probably would.

"Hi." Oh, wait, she'd said that already, hadn't she?

She hadn't seen or spoken to him since their dinner date, but she'd sure thought about him. She'd even broken down and told Meka everything. Including that he'd given her one sizzling kiss and then somehow managed to imply that the kiss was a devious move on her part.

"Well." She cleared her throat. Good, at least one of them had managed something besides hi. Progress was being made. "I assume you showed up to prove that Brad is pocketing the proceeds instead of giving them to charity as claimed?"

He winced, which surprised her. Considering the mood she was in, she wouldn't have minded a good fight. They still had about an hour before the festival was open for business, plenty of time to give Nathan a piece of her mind without frightening guests.

"Sheryl, about the other night...I made a mistake."

"Yes. We covered that already."

"Not the kiss, what I said afterwards. I was out of line."

Hmm. Did that mean he didn't think their kiss was a mistake? In which case, would he be willing to do it again? After all, they still had about an hour before—

Get ahold of yourself. You do not want to kiss this man again.

Well, she shouldn't want to, anyway, not when she knew he'd find the first possible reason to suspect her of something underhanded.

"I'm sorry, Sheryl."

She sighed. So few men were willing to apologize—could she really stay mad at one who was? Especially when he smelled so good, she thought, breathing in his cologne.

"Apology accepted."

"Great." His wide smile warmed places in her she hadn't realized were cold and empty. "Then we can put this behind us and have a terrific day?"

"'Terrific' might be a tad optimistic," she warned, remembering her other non-Nathan problems. "Today's got disaster written all over it. Although I suppose I should find a way to say *disaster* with a more positive spin."

"Anything I can do to help?"

"Thanks, but I doubt it. You're too broad for the elf costume."

The green-and-red-striped shirt would never fit across his well-muscled chest, and he didn't have the scrawny legs of the now-absent teenage boy, so the Christmas-patterned lederhosen wouldn't work, either. A shame, considering that seeing Nathan in the ridiculous outfit might help curb her lust. Or lead to un-precedented lederhosen fantasies and an eventual nervous breakdown.

"You're missing an elf?" he asked.

She nodded. "And a couple hundred hot dogs. But, hey, it's not all bad. Ask me about buns." Nathan's expression turned wolfish, and she hastily amended, "Not my buns. *His.*"

Following her line of sight, he shook his head. "Sorry, not remotely my type. Now, your buns, on the other hand..." He slowly circled her, and she found herself turning, too, so that he couldn't get a backside view. She even briefly considered placing her clipboard over her butt, wishing she hadn't been so busy she'd forgotten to put her jacket back on when she'd left the HGS booth.

This was silly. The ankle-length soft wool skirt she wore with her sweater was hardly transparent. He wasn't going to see anything dozens of people who walked by today couldn't see. But the intensity in his gaze, belying his otherwise playful expression, made it easy to believe he had X-ray vision.

Deciding to go on the offensive and see how *he* liked it, she craned her neck. "While we're on the subject, maybe we should see how yours rate," she threatened.

Faster than Santa's nine reindeer jetting off into the sky, Nathan whipped his body around to accommodate her. "I show you mine, you show me yours—that how you want to play it?"

"No, I was just kid—"

"Should I lift my jacket so you get a better view?" He wiggled his hips a little. "Maybe flex something?"

Her face burned, but laughter bubbled up in her anyway, making her temporarily forget her rotten mood. She had to get him to stop before someone notice his outrageous exhibition. "Would you just cut it out? I have no interest in your buns."

"Hey, I wouldn't voluntarily shake my booty just for anyone." Another wiggle punctuated his statement.

"Honestly, you're like a child. I'm not even looking, you know."

He tossed a knowing smirk over his shoulder. "Liar."

"Sheryl, am I interrupting something?" Grace asked, approaching her boss with two cups of coffee, her eyebrows raised in question.

"Um, no," Sheryl answered, gratefully accepting the coffee. "I was telling Nathan about some of the competitions we hold at the festival, and he was suggesting that for next year we, uh, have some sort of dance contest."

"Uh-huh." Grace's eyes narrowed in skepticism. She either didn't buy Sheryl's story or she thought Nathan should do himself a favor and not enter. Nonetheless, she removed her own clipboard from under her arm and jotted down something about a dance contest. "Anything else you want me to put on the agenda for next year?"

"Yeah." Sheryl caught Nathan's eye, realizing that her grin matched his. His uncharacteristically light-hearted mood was infectious. Today might just turn out all right. "Next year, remind me to schedule a hot dog vendor who actually sells hot dogs."

SHERYL SCANNED the ever-darkening festival area. Today's rousing success meant a nice chunk of money had been raised for numerous area families, so she was entitled to feel her usual post-festival satisfied exhaustion. Instead she felt antsy as she searched for Nathan, whom she'd lost track of as afternoon stretched into evening.

For the duration of the morning, he'd stayed nearby, not interfering with her job in any way, just *being* there. He'd even offered to fill in when they'd needed an extra man on the panel to judge the "draw your favorite video game hero contest."

Though she wasn't normally a person who liked the feeling of someone looking over her shoulder or dogging her steps, she'd liked knowing he was around. She'd been busy working and he'd often been talking to people in the crowd, but every once in a while she'd look up and catch his eye and it was as if everyone else around them disappeared for a moment. While she was surprised that Brad actually seemed to be avoiding Nathan, she'd been happy her boss stayed away, alleviating potential stress between her and Nathan.

They'd eaten lunch together, discovering that they were both cinema buffs with quite a few favorite movies in common, though she despaired of his automatically classifying anything with Charlize Theron a "must-see." Sometime after that, Sheryl had been notified of a technical difficulty in one of the booths, and as she'd arranged to have the problem fixed, she'd lost sight of the man who'd inexplicably become her visual touchstone.

Now, the majority of guests were headed home. A final few were still purchasing last-minute arts, crafts and Christmas presents, while others lingered around the technology booths asking questions or finishing game play. But most of the people bustling about were volunteers and HGS employees, who were helping to take all the booths and decorations down.

Normally the first to arrive and last to leave, Sheryl oversaw wrap-up. This year, though, Grace had volunteered, freeing Sheryl to make the drive to her parents and the dinner for which she was woefully late. Nothing left to do except gather her stuff and leave...but she hated the idea of going without saying goodbye to Nathan.

Unless he'd already left, without saying goodbye to her?

She sighed, her warm breath creating a little cloud of visible irritation in the cold air. Huddling deeper in the confines of her jacket, she crossed between two office buildings to where she'd parked her car. As soon as she climbed inside, she pulled out her cell phone to recharge it as she drove and turned the key in the ignition. Nothing.

Sheryl frowned. No doubt the cold had lulled her little car into hibernation. She tried again to turn over the engine. *Thwacka thwacka thwacka.*

Oh, no. She knew that sound... Hadn't she heard it a couple of weeks ago, before Nathan Hall had entered her life, back when he'd only been a byline and a professional annoyance?

Giving the engine one last try, she jerked the key toward her, knowing even as she did so that her grace period had run out. How had she let herself get so preoccupied that she'd forgotten to call a mechanic? This time the *thwacka* was accompanied by an ominous burning smell. Her car jumped, then shuddered to a complete standstill, eerily silent without even the admonishing *thwacka* to chastise her for automobile neglect.

She reached for her phone. Should she try the auto club first, or her mother, who would no doubt cluck and fuss and ask her why she didn't have regular tune-ups?

Auto club. Definitely.

She punched in the number on her member card and was greeted by a cheery holiday message asking her to hold. Just as she was beginning to wonder why she was waiting in her car instead of returning to the comfort of the space heaters one parking lot over, she heard a tap against her window. Startled, she glanced to her left and discovered the welcome sight of Nathan's face on the other side of the glass.

Opening her door, she said, "I figured you'd left a while ago."

"Without saying goodbye?" His tone was both surprised and slightly accusing. "I wouldn't have done that. I got caught up interviewing one of the families you helped today, but I thought we... How come you're sitting in the parking lot?"

"My car doesn't seem inclined to go anywhere," she admitted. "I'm on hold with the auto club."

"Didn't you have some sort of family thing tonight?"

She nodded. "Dinner at my folks'. I'm sure they're all waiting on me."

"You might be waiting a couple hours on the auto club," Nathan predicted. "Are you against locking up your car and leaving it here? I could take you to your parents', and you could get the car towed to a garage in the morning."

Sounded reasonable. And if someone stole her car during the night—not that they'd get far—well, the insurance money she'd collect was probably of greater value than the vehicle itself.

"You really don't mind driving me?"

His grin was somewhat lopsided, making him look boyish, like the most sought after teenager in the senior class. Which maybe explained her high school urge to pull him into the back seat and have her way with him.

"Your parents don't live in Portland or anything, do they?"

"No, they've got a lovely place in Idaho."

"Wise ass," he muttered, imbuing the term with more genuine affection than Brad had ever managed with his cloying endearments.

She returned his grin. "They're on the other side of downtown."

"You stay here, I'll go pull my car around," Nathan told her.

"You aren't parked here?"

"No, I just jogged over this way because Grace said I might still be able to catch you if I hurried." Again the slightly accusing reminder that she'd been ready to head off without finding him first.

But she was so pleased by his determination to talk to her that she couldn't manage any contrition.

As he disappeared into the darkness, Sheryl revised her original inclination to sell her car for parts. Instead, she patted the dashboard with sincere gratitude.

"You pull through this," she whispered to the lifeless automobile, "and my Christmas present to you is premium gasoline all next year."

NATHAN SHOOK his head as he flipped the blinker on and turned down the street Sheryl had indicated. "You really didn't like that movie? It was critically acclaimed, won an Oscar even."

"It's so bleak. What do you have against happy endings?" Sheryl challenged. "Admit it, you only liked it because Charlize Theron was in it."

He shot an amused glance her way. "You think you have me all figured out, huh?"

She brushed a strand of hair back behind her ear, looking nervous suddenly. "Maybe I'm starting to."

Feeling uncertain himself, he understood her tentative expression. In the past he'd been proud of assessing people quickly, having an eye for detail and knowing how to ask the obscure yet telling questions most people wouldn't have considered. But it had been a while since he'd allowed himself to get to know someone on a really personal level.

After only a short time, he knew how to make Sheryl laugh, knew from the glint in her green eyes when she was getting riled and when she was just teasing. He knew her perfume, her family history, her determination and talent. He was starting to learn how she liked her coffee, although she had so many different favorite blends and varieties, he suspected it would take a lifetime to catalog them all.

A lifetime.

Had he ever considered staying with a person that long? With many people, their families were the most permanent fixtures in their lives. After his mom's abandonment and his dad's death, Nathan didn't seek out a lot of permanence. And he'd met too few people with qualities that inspired him to change.

"This is it, the end of the line," Sheryl declared.

He brushed away the strangely pensive thoughts that clung to him like powdered sugar off the festival's funnel cakes. She was pointing to a two-story house outlined in twinkling white lights. A large evergreen tree stood on one side of the yard, decorated with oversize, brightly colored orbs. Weathered figurines depicting the manger scene sat on the other side of the sidewalk leading up to the front door.

"That one?" he asked.

She nodded. "We've had the same Christmas decorations for as long as I can remember. Dad used to put the nativity underneath the decorated tree, but one year, a ball fell and knocked Joseph unconscious. Figuratively speaking."

Nathan grinned, trying to remember Christmas decorations from his childhood. He rarely bothered with decorations now. Last year he'd helped Kaylee and Frank trim their tree, but why decorate his apartment for just a few weeks when no one would see it? Maybe it would be nice to get a little Christmas tree, though, just a small tabletop one.

He stopped the car at the curb in front of the Dayton house, since the driveway was already filled with an assortment of sedans and minivans. Sheryl had phoned her parents en route to explain the delay, and during the call had confirmed her original suspicion that everyone else was assembled and waiting on her.

No sooner had he shifted into Park than the front door of the house opened—obviously her family had been watching for her. A rounder, silver-haired version of Sheryl bustled down the sidewalk toward them, her Kiss the Cook apron visible beneath an unbuttoned coat.

"You're here!" Mrs. Dayton exclaimed. "They're saying it might snow later, and we were worried. Come in, you two, come in."

You two?

Nathan shot Sheryl an uncertain look. He'd figured someone from her family would take her home later, and that his role was just to drop her off. "I..." He wasn't sure how to refuse her mother's invitation.

Sheryl stilled in the act of unfastening her seat belt. "You're staying, aren't you? You drove me out here, the least we can do is feed you. Just beware of my younger sister's holiday punch. It seems harmless because you can't really taste the vodka, but a cousin had a bit too much one Thanksgiving and wasn't heard from again until Valentine's."

Actually, a stiff drink didn't sound all that unwelcome. He almost never met the families of women he was actually dating, much less doing whatever he and Sheryl were doing.

"Did you have other plans tonight?" she pressed.

No. No, he didn't. He probably would have spent the time alone with the evening news and a microwaved meal like the ones he'd grown up on. Suddenly, an image of his dad superimposed itself over Nathan's picture of himself. Was he turning into his father?

In some ways, Nathan had worked to become the type of man his dad had been. But...though the older Hall had seemed to have a great sense of purpose, he'd never really seemed happy.

"I would love to join your family for dinner." Nathan whipped the safety belt away from his body as though it had been strangling him.

Sheryl smiled. "I'm glad."

They both got out of the car, and she introduced him to her mother, Patricia. By this time, Sheryl's father had also wandered out of the house to kiss his daughter, size up her escort and grumble that the food was getting cold on the table.

Before he knew it, Nathan found himself seated at a wide oak dining room table full of the adults in

Sheryl's family. A couple of younger children sat at a nearby folding card table, chattering away, and Sheryl's youngest niece, only a few months old, slept in a bassinet. Colleen, Sheryl's older sister and the infant's mother, predicted that as soon as the food was served, the baby would wake up screaming for attention.

"It's like she has an internal clock that prevents me from eating a meal in peace," Colleen complained, though Nathan noted that she glanced in the direction of the bassinet every few minutes with obvious love and pride.

In fact, the whole family behaved that way. Sheryl, her sisters and brother, Tom, heckled each other mercilessly, but as soon as an in-law or boyfriend joined in, the same person who'd started the taunting in the first place would suddenly be defending their erstwhile victim. It was easy to see where Sheryl got her fierce sense of loyalty from.

He found himself wondering what it would be like to go through life with a woman like that. A woman you knew would never walk away.

Ridiculous, he told himself even as he formed the thought. He didn't need protection from anything in his life. Unless he listened to Kaylee.

Was loneliness something you needed protection from?

12

A FEW HOURS LATER, despite Patricia's fervent checking of the Weather Channel, snow did not seem to be forthcoming. Sheryl's brother and his wife had bundled their children into the appropriate minivan, and Colleen was upstairs, taking care of diaper duty so that her family could leave, too. Her husband, David, was stomping around, insisting there was no way on God's green earth they were stepping foot outside the house until they found the baby's teething medication or the rest of the night would be insufferable.

Nathan would have joined the search, but he wasn't really sure what he was looking for, and Sheryl, though smiling at her family and still exchanging the occasional teasing barb, appeared ready to fall asleep where she stood. With the festival earlier today, she was bound to be tired, and he felt a protective urge to get her home and tucked into bed. But that's where the urge stopped being so much protective and turned into something completely different.

"It was nice meeting you," Sheryl's younger sister, Lisa, told him as she waited in the foyer. Apparently her boyfriend's car was slow to heat up, and he was outside now with the engine running. "Hope we see you again, Nathan."

He shook her hand, thanking her for her kind thoughts. The whole family, close-knit as they obviously were, had immediately made him feel as though he belonged. There had been no suspicious scrutiny, no sense that he was being judged on his potential flaws. They'd just opened their arms and plied him with roast beef and meringue pie.

In fact, that was the main reason he and Sheryl were still in the foyer instead of in his car and on their way back across the city. Patricia Dayton had insisted they couldn't go anywhere until she'd put a couple of slices of pie into a plastic container for Nathan to take with him.

Lisa turned her attention from Nathan to Sheryl. "Chad should have the car warm enough by now. See you Christmas Day, sis." With that, she bounced out the door and down the sidewalk, leaving Sheryl and Nathan alone in the lamp-lit foyer.

"You look beat," Nathan observed.

But somehow even exhaustion flattered her. Sleepiness had softened her features, and her eyes were only half-open. Full, dark lashes fluttered over gentle green pools, and her mouth was parted in yielding invitation.

She leaned against him. "I think I'm ready to hit the sack."

Her muffled yawn made him feel bad for his wayward thoughts, but could he help it that her body was pliant and curvaceous against his? He anchored her with one arm around her slim waist, but shot a glance ceilingward, seeking restraint from any further touches.

So much for help from that quarter. Above them, cheerily bedecked with red velvet ribbon, was a sprig of mistletoe that he hadn't noticed until now.

Alone with Sheryl underneath mistletoe.

He wasn't sure what small sound or movement he

must have made that gave him away, but suddenly Sheryl moved from her relaxed near-sprawl against him. She was looking up, too, as though checking to see what had captured his attention.

"Oh." Her breath escaped in the barely audible word. "It's, um, mistletoe."

A holiday tradition. And after the way she'd talked about the lawn decorations her family had put out for years and the way she'd talked about Santa with the kids at the festival, he bet Sheryl honored holiday traditions.

The change in her expression confirmed his suspicion. Her eyes were still fluttering between open and closed, and her lips were still parted. But there was nothing remotely sleepy in her appearance now.

Bending his head, he took the opportunity he'd been subconsciously looking for all day. His lips captured hers, on a sensual mission to erase their last kiss with this one, to make up for the way he'd bungled things. The tartness of lemon meringue couldn't quite block the sweetness of her flavor, and Nathan slanted his mouth across hers, wanting more. She sucked gently on his lower lip, and his body throbbed with need.

With one hand cupped behind her head, he tried to bring her even closer, so that he could breathe her in, surround himself in her. But he knew that no kiss would be enough to satisfy his craving for her. He wanted her around him in ways that would be entirely inappropriate in her parents' foyer.

"Ahem." A man cleared his throat.

Speaking of her parents' foyer... Nathan pulled back, an unfamiliar heat in his face. Good grief, he wasn't *blushing*, was he?

Sheryl's smirking brother-in-law held out a clear

container filled with pie. His expression was stern, but he couldn't quite hide the mischief in his gaze. "Patricia wanted me to deliver this while she helped look for the baby's pain reliever. But seems to me like you two had something different on your minds for dessert."

"YOU TWO HAVE a nice night," Mrs. Dayton said from the curb. Nathan couldn't quite meet the woman's gaze as he held open the passenger door for Sheryl. Hard to thank Mrs. Dayton for her hospitality when he was more preoccupied with imagining her daughter naked.

"Oh, I'm *sure* they will," David said pointedly. He had followed them to the car, hinting that he'd found them making out like teenagers in the foyer. Mr. Dayton had raised his eyebrows. As far as Nathan could tell, Mrs. Dayton was pretending not to understand the insinuations.

Once Nathan was seated inside the car, the Daytons safely on the other side of closed doors, he turned to Sheryl. But he had no idea what to say.

Should he apologize? He wasn't sorry at all that he'd kissed her, only that her siblings were no doubt going to tease her about this.

She took a deep breath. "So...last time you kissed me, you claimed to have made a mistake. And this time?"

This time he wanted to pull the car off the road and kiss her some more. But she'd been right in that parking garage. If they were going to pursue this—and letting it go was *not* an option—they should talk.

For a man who made his living with words, he suddenly found they'd all deserted him. "Sheryl...I, um, I'm very attracted to you."

Instead of bruising his ego, her laugh helped break the tension. "You know, I was starting to get that idea."

"You were right before, that we should discuss your job. And my job." He didn't mention Hammond by name, because there was no room in this car for anyone but Nathan and Sheryl. Not even in conversation.

"Can we keep our professional and private lives separate?" she asked. She said "we" but he got the impression she really meant *you*.

"I don't want to date your employer," he assured her. "So what's been done or not isn't as important as your being honest with me. Which isn't to say I think you've ever lied," he hastily added, lest he sabotage the progress they seemed to be making. "But I won't lie to you, either, and you know I have my doubts about this lawsuit."

She considered this. "So we agree to disagree? You can continue to harbor your doubts, but we don't discuss the case. And in return, you continue to get nothing but honesty from me. Sound like a plan?" When he nodded, she said, "You realize we should seal this deal with a kiss?"

Happy to oblige, he rapidly followed her instructions to her apartment complex and tried to keep at least some of the blood from draining from his brain in the meantime.

No sooner had they reached her parking lot, than he threw the gear shift into Park and yanked the keys out of the ignition. Sheryl had already fumbled her way free of the seat belt and was leaning across the armrest to meet him. They came together in a fiery kiss that was more than enough to heat the inside of the car.

Flames of desire licked at Nathan's blood, sending a

roar through his ears that must have been the sound of sheer wanting. He pulled her closer, luxuriating in the feel of her mouth on his, but wanting to kiss her everywhere else, too. Ducking, he nibbled at her neck, learned the delicate curves of her ear, sought out the places where she was most sensitive.

While he explored the honeyed taste and satiny texture of her skin, Sheryl's hands frantically roamed his body. She seemed to be in the same condition he was—wanting to touch everywhere at once, not sure where to start. Her hands scraped down his back, tangled through his hair, cupped his face as she kissed him with every bit of passion he'd always known she had in her.

Angling his body to try to pull her closer, he jammed the steering console with his elbow. The resultant blare of the horn made them spring apart, both panting for air.

Sheryl pressed a hand to her cheek, her eyes round. "N-now I'm glad no one in my family walked in on *that*."

Though it cost him the little breath he'd managed to catch, Nathan laughed. Laughing with Sheryl was almost as good as kissing her...but not quite.

"I think maybe I'm too old to make out in cars," she said finally.

He opened his door, needing the fresh, cool air to clear his spinning head. "Come on, I'll walk you upstairs."

No gentleman would do any less. What happened when they got there would depend on her.

Not trusting himself to speak—rather, not trusting himself not to beg her to let him make love to her until morning—he enfolded her hand with his, lacing their fingers together, and silently walked her inside the building and up to her apartment. Strangely, the small contact between them was even more intimate than what had happened in the car. Anyone could lust after someone else, but you only held hands with someone you truly liked.

She put the key in her door and lifted her chin, meeting his gaze. If she invited him in, it didn't necessarily mean they would make love, but given their mutual conditions... As she pushed the door open, he swallowed.

Before either of them could say anything, a female voice called a cheery, "Hi!" from somewhere inside a dimly lit living room. The only illumination came from the television set and the soft glow of a Christmas tree decorated in blue blinking lights and silver tinsel.

Fighting the urge to grind his teeth, Nathan glanced past Sheryl to find an attractive black woman waggling her fingers at them from the couch where she sat curled in a man's arms. The tender possessiveness with which they held each other, the contentment obvious in their expressions even in the shadowed room, made him think of Kaylee and Frank.

He turned back to Sheryl, whose rueful smile conveyed her own disappointment and a silent apology. It wouldn't be unheard of for the two of them to just head back to Sheryl's room and ignore the roommate, but that was a big presumption on Nathan's part. Besides, he'd heard Sheryl talk enough about growing up with siblings and her resulting need for privacy to know that idea might not appeal to her.

"Nathan," Sheryl began, "this is my roommate and best friend, Tameka Williams, and her boyfriend, Tyler

McAfee. Guys, this is Nathan. He drove me home because my car wouldn't start."

"Nice to meet you," Nathan said, even though part of him was chagrined at being dismissed as nothing more than a chauffeur. Did that mean he was going to be denied the chance to kiss Sheryl good-night?

"I'll, um, see you around?" he asked her, not sure where they went from here and not wanting to figure it out in front of the couple now watching them instead of the television. He angled his body toward the door and clasped his car keys, going through the motions of a man departing without actually making any progress in that direction.

"What are your plans on Friday?" Sheryl asked him softly. "I mean, will you be out of town for Christmas, or—"

"Just spending the afternoon with Kaylee and Frank and a few of Frank's friends from the force." Other unmarried guys Kaylee had adopted and worried over.

A grin split his face. She could lecture *them* now, because Nathan's problem had been resolved. His friend had accused him of keeping others at arm's length, but he wanted Sheryl as close as he could get her. In every sense.

She leaned in, her body language indicating that she was displeased to have an audience, then whispered, "I'm spending Christmas Day with my family, but...I could come back here that night. Tameka is taking Ty to meet her parents. Would you, um, would you like to have a late dinner with me?"

The unmistakable heat in her gaze made him weak.

"I'll be here." The promise spilled out of his dry mouth in a low, shaky tone, but his absolute conviction that there was nowhere else he'd rather be came through.

Then he couldn't help himself any longer—audience or no audience. He cupped his fingers over her shoulders and hauled her against him, kissing her in an old-movie reenactment, the kind where the man takes charge with a powerful kiss and the woman kicks up her foot behind her as dramatic music swells in the background. So what if the background music in this instance was the opening theme to a late-night talk show?

Reluctantly releasing Sheryl, he offered a jaunty little wave to the now-gaping Tameka and Ty. Sheryl's soft, breathy "Wow" followed him to the front door, and he almost laughed at the idea of driving his car home. He felt like he could fly instead.

IT WAS MIDMORNING Monday when Sheryl finally realized she hadn't had a single drop of caffeine all day. And yet she felt amazing. Ordinarily, her coffee-free state would transform her into Dr. Jeckyll's less friendly other half. In her unprecedented good mood, she should probably find poor Elliot and get their postponed conversation about Grace out of the way once and for all.

She'd commuted to work with a serene smile not even inconsiderate freeway drivers could dislodge, and when she'd bid Denise good morning, her own cheerfulness had actually rivaled the receptionist's.

I'm falling in love.

She gripped the edge of the desk and dropped the rest of the weekend mail she'd been sorting through, waiting. But though she might have expected some earth-shattering reaction, admitting her feelings for

Nathan didn't make it impossible for her to continue standing in front of her desk. As she gave it a moment to sink in, she realized she wasn't actually shocked. How could she be?

Hadn't she been more and more drawn to him over the past few weeks, more willing to open up bits of herself? On some level, she had to have known what her growing emotions signified.

No, the realization was more like a gentle sigh. Her entire body relaxed, happy that she wasn't going to try to deny or fight her feelings. The only thing that could possibly add any tension now was...could he love her? She suspected that men were slower to acknowledge and act on their emotions.

Fine by her. She wasn't looking for any undying declarations by the end of the week, necessarily. But could they have a future together?

Maybe she was just feeling overly optimistic, but after this weekend, she truly thought so. He'd seemed so free-spirited at the festival, and after dinner with her family—with whom any reasonable human being could find fault—he'd had nothing but nice things to say. The man who'd once snidely informed her that he wasn't so gullible to take a person's kindness at face value hadn't been in evidence this weekend. The thought gave her hope.

Grace poked her head into Sheryl's office. "Hey, Brad wanted me to send you to the conference room. He's called a meeting, and he seemed pretty agitated."

Sheryl frowned, but she supposed that they paid her to actually work and not stand around fantasizing about a guy. "On my way."

Grace hadn't been exaggerating when she'd described their boss as "agitated." He was pacing the length of the conference room, furrowing both hands through his hair. Mark Campbell sat nearby, his face grim. The rest of the company's management was represented, and Sheryl slid into a vacant chair next to Wyce Brown.

Mark nodded his acknowledgement of Sheryl's presence and launched right into what he needed to say. "Settling with Kendra Mathers hasn't worked, and the case has merits. Looks like she'll get her day in court after all, and a date will be set for after Christmas. Sheryl, there will probably be renewed mention of this in the media now, so you and I need to get together to discuss some strategy. You have time this afternoon?"

"Absolutely." Rather, she'd make time. Renewed mention in the media...she refused to think about what that might mean for her personal life. The case was professional, and it had nothing to do with her feelings for Nathan. Nonetheless, the sinking sensation in the pit of her stomach warned that this wasn't going to be the right day to impress Elliot Loomis with her sunny disposition, after all.

The brief meeting, though unfortunate, wasn't entirely unexpected. They'd all known this was a strong possibility. But until now, she'd never seen Brad so frazzled by it. Had he just been in denial the whole time, refusing to admit this would make it to trial? Or was something more bothering him?

As Mark headed off for an appointment and her co-workers trailed out of the office, she hung back a little until she was alone with her employer.

"How are you holding up?" she asked him.

"Rough weekend. There was a phone call yesterday..."

She'd expected him to say something about the

meeting they'd just concluded, not a phone call. Were the two connected, or was something else bothering him? "A phone call from Mark?"

"No, a woman. She... Never mind."

"What woman?"

"You know what? It'll be fine." He squared his shoulders. "You're going to have enough to worry about, and this would just upset you."

Uh-oh. "Why? What would upset me?"

"It's probably nothing anyway." He didn't seem to be talking to her now, but to himself. "It will all be fine. Right, Sheryl?"

Without waiting for an answer, he strode from the conference room, leaving her confused and craving a double shot of espresso.

"Well, that was weird," she said to the empty room.

A woman? Maybe it was some sort of relationship thing and he wasn't seeking Sheryl's advice now because she'd always refused to entwine their employer-employee relationship with their romantic past. But as far as she knew, Brad had been too busy with the company and the holidays to pursue anyone romantically. He'd had a date earlier this month, but had reported that "they hadn't clicked" and had come alone to the Christmas party.

No, she couldn't help feeling that what Brad was upset about was this case. And that the troubling phone call yesterday was linked to it.

For the very first time since Kendra Mathers had popped up out of the woodwork, an inkling of doubt wormed its way through Sheryl. Did Brad know something he wasn't telling her? Had Brad...*done* something she didn't know about? Something that would explain the almost hunted expression in his eyes?

Dismissing the thought as both traitorous and impossible, she stormed out of the conference room. Brad wasn't guilty of anything except the occasional lack of common sense. Definitely time to find herself some caffeine and then dive into her morning so that there'd be extra time for her meeting with Mark this afternoon.

As she passed through the reception area, Denise held up her hand, signaling that Sheryl should wait nearby until Denise concluded her current phone call.

Pausing, Sheryl noted the array of fresh, beautiful flowers on Denise's desk. They brightened the entire room.

Denise transferred the caller to customer service and moved her headset aside. "Just the woman I needed to see."

Sheryl cocked her head toward the bouquet. "From Joe?"

"No, actually. They were delivered for you while you were in your meeting."

"Me?" Sheryl grinned, hoping that she wasn't about to open the card and find they were from an organization HGS had helped raise funds and awareness for on Saturday. She grasped the small blue envelope that peeked out from amid the rosebuds and tore it open.

Sheryl—
Can't stop thinking about you. Or your buns. See you Christmas.

                                              Nathan

Her laugh trilled through the quiet area, and Denise raised her eyebrows.

"From your newspaper man?"

Sheryl nodded.

How would Denise feel about that? She wasn't exactly a fan of Nathan Hall, nor were many of Sheryl's other co-workers.

But Denise grinned slyly. "So things are taking off between the two of you?"

"We're spending Christmas together." Christmas night, at least. The time between now and Friday seemed to stretch on forever. She hadn't been so impatient for Christmas to get here since she was a kid.

"Clever girl," Denise said. "Guess there's more than one way to get him to listen to our side of things, isn't there?"

Sheryl stiffened. The receptionist didn't mean anything by her comment, but still...now that the case was going to court, would it hurt her budding relationship with Nathan?

He cared about his job as much as she did hers, probably more, given his zeal for honesty and journalistic integrity. That job might require him to write about her company in the near future. Could she handle that?

The tiny twinge of doubt she'd experienced in the conference room haunted her. If she didn't believe in her friend, how could she expect Nathan to? And how would she feel if he insisted on her friend's guilt?

Chiding herself to stop borrowing trouble, she clung to the pact she and Nathan had made. *Jobs are not relationships. The two things can be kept separate.*

She hoped.

13

"I AM A BAD PERSON," Sheryl told her reflection in the mirrored closet door. It wasn't that she hadn't enjoyed her morning with her family—she loved this special holiday and sharing it with those closest to her—but she was glad to be home. By midafternoon, when the kids had fallen into exhausted naps and everyone was fussing over her newly engaged sister, Sheryl had begun stealing glances at her watch, wondering how soon she could leave.

Today had been the first Christmas engagement for the Dayton family. When her brother had proposed to his wife years ago, he'd told his family in advance. They'd wished him luck, then welcomed his fiancée to the clan after the engagement was official. Sheryl had been happy for him. Then when her older sister had later announced at a family dinner that she was engaged, Sheryl had been happy again.

Happy, but aware her mother was shooting her speculative are-you-next? glances.

Today, when Sheryl should have been thrilled for her baby sister, she'd instead retreated into her own world. She'd imagined for the first time what it would be like to come home and tell her family *she* had found The One. Not long ago, Sheryl had told Meka this wasn't a good time for romance in her life. It was a time for career advancement, for putting herself first, which she couldn't do in a healthy relationship.

She'd meant all of that when she'd said it.

But that was before Nathan had admitted another man paying attention to her made him jealous. Before window-shopping for Christmas toys. Before his booty-shaking demonstration that had made her laugh on a morning when all she'd wanted to do was cry in frustration. Before she'd realized that she was trapped in a cycle of the-more-she-saw-him-the-more-she-wanted-to-see-him.

And she couldn't wait to see him tonight.

She was relieved her still-celebrating sister hadn't minded that Sheryl left early. She'd worked in some extra cooing over the diamond ring to atone, but how was she supposed to have known her sister would pick today to get engaged? Sheryl couldn't cancel her plans with Nathan, and she had been looking forward to the two of them making the most of Tameka's absence.

Plopping down on her bed, she thought about that. Now, she wanted her own place more than ever, but she no longer wanted to be alone. Today, surrounded by all those happy couples, thinking about the impending evening with the man she loved... Being alone was overrated.

She just hadn't realized it before because she'd never actually *been* alone.

"Okay, enough of this." No time for soul-searching when she had dinner preparations to tackle and the looming all-important question of what the heck should she wear?

She wanted something sexy but not overly forward. Just because she was pretty sure she knew what was going to happen between them tonight didn't mean she had to answer the door in an outfit that screamed "bedroom's thataway, big guy." Obviously, she wanted to look her best, but they were having dinner in her apartment, so no sense in dressing formally. And if she didn't decide something soon, she wasn't going to have time to make the risotto.

She'd spoken briefly to Nathan on the phone this morning, unable to keep the breathless anticipation out of her voice as she'd thanked him for the flowers now sitting on her nightstand and confirmed what time he should be here. Smiling a little, she recalled that he'd sounded plenty eager himself.

And since he was looking forward to this evening as much as she was, she didn't want to disappoint. She owed it to him to pick out some clothes and make the best dinner she could. Her red dress was the most flattering thing she owned, but she'd feel like an idiot slinking around her kitchen in it. Did slacks have the right at-home feel?

Forget slacks. Tonight definitely called for a skirt.

The phone rang on her nightstand, and she jumped.

"Hello?"

"Merry Christmas, girl."

"Hey, Meka. You and Ty get in safely?" They'd flown out yesterday to stay with Meka's mom and stepfather and would leave tomorrow to meet up with Tameka's dad in Cincinnati before coming home on Thursday.

"Yeah, Mom's crazy about him already. I won't keep you," Meka promised, a smirk in her tone. "I know you have plans, and we're about to go out to dinner."

"There's a place open on Christmas Day?" Sheryl asked incredulously.

"Mom always makes sure in advance. Can't cook to save her life. But I had to wish you a happy holiday."

"Thanks. Merry Christmas to you, too. Both of you."

"Oh, and why don't you borrow my dark blue skirt? The short one? It'll be a tiny bit more modest on you and look great with that sweater I got you for your birthday."

Sheryl did a quick mental review of Meka's closet and paired the suggested skirt and sweater. "Perfect! What would I do without you?"

"Lord only knows." Her roommate chuckled. "I'll see you in a couple of days."

Wishing her roommate safe travel, Sheryl said goodbye, already pulling her long-sleeved T-shirt over her head to exchange for the aqua-yellow-and-navy-striped cropped sweater. Meka was a genius! And now that Sheryl had the outfit decided on, everything else would fall into place.

EVERYTHING WAS A DISASTER! When the instructions said do not stop stirring the risotto, they meant do *not* stop stirring the risotto. Sheryl shoved the pan into the sink, disgusted with herself. But she'd had to stop stirring in order to change her top. *Note to self—next time planning romantic evening, make food before putting on perfect outfit, so as not to stain sweater.*

Nothing else looked quite as good with Meka's skirt, but by the time Sheryl'd realized this, the risotto was stuck to the pan. Adding insult to injury, the flaky croissants in the oven had burned, too. Though perhaps not entirely inedible, they'd definitely passed that golden-brown stage and headed toward Cajun, blackened territory. If she were serving them with gumbo, she could probably pull it off.

"At least I can't ruin the salad," she mumbled, heading back to her bedroom. She still didn't know what to wear, but just to finish the cooking preparations, she paired a basketball T-shirt with faded, button-fly jeans, not even bothering to button them all the way since she'd find a new skirt after she'd prepared the salmon.

Back in the kitchen, she realized she was missing one of the spices she'd been certain Meka had in stock. She glared at the clock on the wall as though it were to blame for her troubles. How had she gone from wishing the time would fly by faster to wishing she could stop it completely? In her rushed nervousness, she burned her hand twice and was considering putting butter on it when the doorbell rang.

No!

He was early. How could he be early?

Telling herself that it would be wrong to ignore the buzzer and pretend no one was home, she scampered across the living room. Maybe he was early because he was so desperate to see her. Desperate enough to overlook her appearance and the rapidly dwindling menu?

She pasted a polite smile on her face as she opened the door, but as soon as she saw Nathan, the edges of her smile softened, becoming real.

"Hi," he said.

"Hi, yourself." For a moment, she lost herself in his eyes. But she knew she should invite him inside, so she took a step back, letting her gaze trail down his body. Then she burst out laughing.

Under his leather jacket, Nathan was wearing a basketball T-shirt with a pair of jeans, an outfit very similar to the one he'd been wearing the first time she'd seen him. And almost identical to what she currently had on.

"We match," she managed to say a second later.

"Well, that is a faux pas. But I know of at least one way we can make sure we're not wearing the same clothes anymore." He punctuated his statement with a wickedly raised eyebrow, and desire uncurled in her abdomen.

Carrying a wrapped package under one arm, he stepped inside. "Sorry I'm early." He set the package on the coffee table and shrugged out of his coat. "I left myself time to go back to my place and change into something nicer, but halfway there I realized I'd feel stupid if I showed up in a coat and tie. And I really couldn't wait to see you. Now I'm glad I didn't dress up."

She glanced woefully at her outfit. "These were my cooking clothes. You weren't supposed to see me like this."

He dropped his jacket on the back of the couch and with his hands now free, pulled her to him for a kiss hello. "You look pretty damn good to me," he murmured against her lips.

They tumbled together to the sofa when the kiss consumed them too much to leave them standing. Suddenly nothing else mattered but having him here. The food, the clothes, the missing seasonings—who cared? Nathan was all the spice she needed.

A small sound escaped her when he pulled away, but he chuckled. "I have something I want to give you."

Oh, baby.

But he reached down and lifted the package she'd noticed earlier. "Merry Christmas, Sheryl."

She bit her lip. "You didn't have to do this. I don't have a gift for you exactly."

"That's okay."

"But I do have..." She rose and went to Meka's carefully decorated Christmas tree against the wall. She and Meka had exchanged gifts a few days ago, so the only presents remaining were two small wrapped boxes.

She returned to the sofa, holding out both hands as she sat down. "I couldn't make up my mind."

"What are they?" Nathan asked.

She laughed. "Usually, you unwrap them to find out. Has no one explained to you how this process works?"

He set one next to him and opened the other, uncovering an elegant Christmas ornament. He stared at the carved, old-fashioned quill pen alongside a tiny resin scroll with a poem about writers. She knew from picking it out at the store that you had to squint to make out the words on the scroll, but the verse was lovely. About how words could be used to reveal the truth and beauty of the world.

He glanced up from the ornament which looked so fragile in his big hands. For a moment, he said nothing, and his true gratitude echoed in the silence. "Thank you. You know what's funny? I just bought a Christmas tree this week, then realized I had virtually nothing to put on it."

Her lips twitched as she nudged the second box toward him. "Now you have at least two. I couldn't decide which one I wanted to get you more."

Shooting her a curious glance, he ripped the paper off the second gift, then threw his head back and laughed when he saw the picture on the box. A collector's edition replica of a miniature soldier wearing fatigues and combat boots.

"I don't believe they made him into a Christmas ornament," he told her. "And that you bought him. Wait'll you see— Open yours now."

She did, eagerly, but not tearing the paper off as he'd done. The uneven folds and taping said that this box had not been professionally wrapped, and she was somehow touched to think of him doing it himself. After she'd carefully peeled away the paper, she pulled out the cardboard-and-plastic box inside, finding the decorative doll she'd admired outside of FAO Schwarz. Golden curls gleamed around a porcelain face with a delicate smile and wide blue eyes that looked so real you expected her to blink or giggle.

Nathan cleared his throat. "I know it's sort of an impractical gif—"

Quickly setting the doll on the coffee table out of harm's way, Sheryl moved forward to press her hand against his mouth. She wouldn't let him unintentionally spoil the moment by downplaying the gift.

Deciding to thank him with actions rather than words, she removed her hand, leaning in to replace it with her mouth. In the second before they kissed, his gaze locked with hers. While she couldn't be certain what her expression was, she was pretty sure it translated to "Bedroom's thataway, big guy."

Their openmouthed kiss was deep and eager. She

locked her arms around him and could only cling to his shoulders when he dragged himself away long enough to nibble at the sensitive flesh of her neck. He dotted light, butterfly kisses up and down her collarbone. One minute dropping a kiss against her jaw, then dipping back to nip at the skin just above the neckline of her shirt.

Eventually—*soon*, she hoped—he'd work his way even lower, beneath her shirt, and her breasts already tingled and tightened with anticipation.

Restless with desire, she slid her hands down and around, underneath the front of his shirt, skimming her fingers over his taught stomach. She felt him shiver beneath her touch, his muscles tightening. Spurred on by his response, she raised her head and lightly bit his earlobe.

His weight suddenly shifted, pushing her back against the sofa. Sheryl didn't mind at all, but the couch was too narrow to allow both of them the maneuverability they needed to continue their frantic discoveries of each other. Nathan pulled back only slightly, keeping his weight pressed against her.

"Will you be terribly offended if we skip dinner?" he asked.

"Well..." For appearance' sake, she pretended to think the question over. Inside, she was doing an end-zone victory dance that he'd handed her an excuse to skip the burned-risotto portion of the evening. "Okay, you talked me into it."

Plan A had been to impress him with her culinary skills. Probably best to move on to Plan B—wow him with her sex goddess imitation. Granted, it had been a while since she'd had sex, but at least she was confident nothing would end up scalded, charred or melted. Reasonably confident, anyway. She made a mental note not to light any candles near the bed.

Even if her risotto had turned out cooking-magazine perfect, she wouldn't have cared about showing it off. The only thing she wanted to devour was the man leaning above her, whose face had become so achingly dear to her she couldn't imagine a time when it hadn't been imprinted on her mind, even though she knew that had been true only last month. A lifetime ago.

He sat up completely, taking away the tantalizing press of his muscled hardness against her softer, now aching body. Then he stood, holding his hands out to her.

She clasped them, thinking he meant to help her to her feet. But he swung her up in his arms and cradled her against his chest instead, eliciting a startled gasp from Sheryl and no small amount of appreciation. Bless the man able to lift you as though you were a mere delicate wisp of a girl who hadn't eaten one too many brownies during the holiday season.

"Which way?" he asked, stealing a quick kiss before she had time to answer.

Melting under the hot adoration in his eyes, she sagged against him, boneless, and tilted her chin toward her bedroom.

Once there, he was gentleman enough not to mention the tornado of discarded clothes strewn across several surfaces, including the floor. Miraculously, nothing cluttered the bed. She'd planned to tidy up before he arrived, but she congratulated her subconscious on leaving the bed free just in case.

His dark-chocolate gaze fell only on the flowers on

her nightstand, and he smiled down at her once again, laying her across the comforter. ''Not nearly as beautiful as you,'' he pronounced, glancing between her and the bouquet.

She twined her arms around him, pulling him to her. The times she'd wanted to touch him since their first date flashed through her mind. Now that she was free to run her fingers through his hair or take his hand, the moments blurred together. Her lips tasted him, her fingers explored the strength of his biceps as he held his weight slightly off of her, her hand slid his shirt off to find the heat of his skin.

Her own shirt had wriggled up substantially while she moved beneath him, and he skimmed his hand over her usually ticklish abdomen. Laughing or squirming away didn't even occur to her. Instead, she merely sucked in her breath as he inched his way up, laying his palm over the spot where her heart fluttered beneath his touch.

Then he slid his hand to the side, cupping her through the silky fabric of her bra, his fingers lightly circling her, teasing her with their whisper of a touch. Only when she was ready to grab his hand and show him where she wanted to be touched, did he brush his thumb over a hardened, aching nipple. *Finally.* No doubt he could read her pleasure in the small moan that escaped her and the way she arched her back to meet him. Seconds later, he removed her shirt and lobbed it through the air to join the other clothes on the floor.

Nathan glanced down at her body, and she thought how awkward this moment could've been. She'd only had a couple of lovers, and the first time anyone saw her naked, she always braced herself, wondering if they were seeing any flaws or had somehow expected more.

But Nathan's eyes held only awe...and slight confusion as his gaze fell on her unfastened jeans. "I don't remember unbuttoning those," he admitted with a grin. "I must be better at this than I thought."

A laugh caught in her throat. She'd explain later, she thought, pulling him back for another kiss and lifting her hips obligingly when he tugged at the denim waistband.

Once he removed her bra, all coherent thought was lost. For a few exquisite minutes—or maybe hours—his fingers and mouth created sensations in her so unbearably, wrenchingly perfect that she couldn't imagine ever wanting anything more. As long as he never stopped what he was doing.

But gradually, she did want more.

The throbbing that seemed to come from the very core of her bordered on pain, and with desperate hands, she helped him work free of his jeans and T-shirt. As good as he'd looked in both casual and dressier clothes, he managed to look even better without them. Later, she might take the time to appreciate the gift of a perfect masculine form, but right now, all she cared about was easing the ache inside her, being with Nathan.

Kissing her again, he rested one hand against her hip, trailing it down over her thigh and to the wet center of her as his tongue thrust into her mouth. Her entire body jerked and quivered. She kissed him back with impatient passion.

He at least still had the necessary motor skills to deal

with the condom—she was sure she was shaking too badly to have been that coordinated. Then meeting her eyes for a second, he slid into her. Having waited for this moment all week, having waited for this man all her life, it didn't take much to send Sheryl spiraling toward the edge.

He let her set the pace as she bucked against him, clutching his forearms as though he were her only anchor. Her body seized and rippled in a joyous cataclysm that left her breathless and blotted out everything else in the world except the two of them.

14

SHERYL AWAKENED SLOWLY, feeling almost as though she were being tickled but not quite. She peeked one eye open and in the early-morning sunlight saw Nathan running a pale pink, feather-soft exotic bloom over her ribs and toward her navel.

"Morning," he said, grinning down at her.

"Already?" She reached up and ran her hand along his slightly roughened jaw.

They'd made love several times during the night, and in the interim had demolished the salad she'd prepared earlier. Nathan had offered to make the famous Nathan Hall Omelette to go with it, but she'd lacked all but one ingredient, so they'd made do with the not-so-famous Nathan Hall Scrambled Eggs. And eventually, they'd slept. Granted, not for very many hours, but it had been a thorough sleep.

Sheryl had never felt more at peace than she did this morning. Her body resonated with a slumberous, bone-deep relaxation that not even the world's best massage could duplicate.

He lifted her hand to press a kiss against her palm. "Would I sound like some kind of lunatic if I said it's nice watching you sleep?"

She managed a drowsy smile as she snuggled underneath the sheets. "A lunatic? No. Just a guy who doesn't require much in the way of active entertainment."

Arching one brow, he grinned. "Just how much more active do you think two people can get?"

"Not much," she admitted. "And not at all until one of us gets a little bit more rest."

He set the flower on the nightstand and pulled her into his arms. "Then sleep a bit more. I'll be here when you wake up."

Sheryl thought they were the nicest words she'd ever heard. *I'll be here...* That was all she needed to be truly content.

When she woke again, Nathan had pulled on his jeans and was setting a cup of coffee on her nightstand. "For you."

"I knew there was a reason I was crazy about you," she said.

"And that's it? Because I brought you coffee? I'm disappointed."

She might have laughed, but she was too busy savoring the French roast he'd already added creamer to and sweetened. A slight rustling let her know he'd also grabbed her morning paper.

"This was outside your door," he told her, handing over today's edition while he sat on the edge of the bed. "I hope you don't mind my reading it first, but I wanted to check some scores and scope out the inferior columnists."

After last night, she'd forgive him a lot more than reading her newspaper before she did. But her smile faltered at the reminder of his column. They'd shared something beautiful, but it was new and fragile. Would it survive the coming court case and whatever Nathan had to write about it?

She took a deep breath. "I know we aren't talking about this, but..." *Leave well enough, alone, Sheryl.*

But she couldn't. Not after last night had been the most amazing thing to ever happen to her. When she and Nathan had originally said that their jobs wouldn't interfere, there hadn't been any new developments. She had to make sure that their deal would hold, even though the case was moving forward and once again be in the public eye.

"The lawsuit is going to court," she said.

If he was surprised she was bringing this up, he hid it well. "I heard that the day before yesterday. You're worried?"

"Not about the case... I mean, that's another subject. After last night, I really don't want anything to spoil—"

"Nothing will. I'm sure my paper will cover the salient points of the trial, but don't worry about me or my column."

Unease rippled through her. Somehow, the reassurance made her feel worse. She'd never set out to come between Nathan and his job.

"Why shouldn't I worry?"

He shrugged, appearing more mellow about the topic than she'd ever seen him. Then again, hours and hours of fantastic sex could relax a person. "My column covers opinions and human interest, not as much of the straight news as what you see on the front pages. And since I've already stated opinions on this subject...well, my editor's not a fan of redundancy."

Was he making her a promise he'd resent her for later?

He reached out to brush his hand over her face, seemingly trying to smooth the frown lines she knew were there. "I was hoping you'd look a little happier. Sheryl, seriously, whatever a judge decides, the only person whose integrity I care about is yours. And you've never misled me or hid anything."

Except for her momentary doubt the other day, she thought, suddenly recalling the weird way Brad had behaved. But that had been an aberration. She didn't really think he was guilty of anything.

She forced a smile. "Sorry I even brought it up. I know that wasn't part of our deal."

He quirked an eyebrow. "Perhaps I can think of a way for you to make it up to me."

It turned out they both had a couple of good ideas on how she might do that. And by the time they'd each had a chance to demonstrate their various thoughts on the subject, the weekend was over.

SHERYL WOKE on Monday with the dim memory of Nathan kissing her goodbye sometime earlier as he left for his own apartment. He'd already brewed coffee, kept warm in the electric pot, and as she drank it, she smiled over his thoughtfulness.

At the office, Denise greeted her with the news that a court date had been set. Everyone at work seemed subdued by the announcement. Sheryl supposed walking around grinning like a woman who'd just had forty-eight hours of the best sex known to humankind was inappropriate. But she needn't have worried. Running into her employer in the breakroom effectively dampened her mood.

Crescent-shaped shadows were visible under Brad's pale blue eyes, and she felt terrible that he obviously hadn't been able to enjoy his holidays.

"Is there anything I can do for you?" she asked as she stirred sugar into her coffee.

His gaze darted back and forth across the room, empty except for the two of them, before he leaned against the counter. "I don't know. You could probably do your job better if I'd... Sheryl, you know *Xandria Quest* was my idea, right? *My* idea?"

"Of course."

"How do you think other people see me?" he asked.

Unsure whether he meant other people within the company or the general public, she went with the safest answer. "All of us at HGS are behind you."

He didn't look relieved. "For now. But suppose information—"

A woman from the accounting department entered, followed by a co-worker sharing a humorous description of all the Christmas Eve assembly required on his kids' gifts this year.

Brad nodded to the newcomers, then told Sheryl, "I should get back to work. Mark's coming to the office to meet me in a little bit anyway."

She nodded, but her uneasiness stayed with her.

After waiting a couple of hours, she decided to drop by Brad's office to see if he wanted to talk more. His receptionist, Iris, had asked for a couple of extra days' vacation to stay with her son, daughter-in-law and new grandbaby, so the executive suite was empty and quiet.

Quiet enough for the conversation Brad was having to spill out of his office, where the door was ajar.

"...it doesn't matter since they can't use it," Mark was saying.

Sheryl hadn't expected the meeting Brad had with their lawyer to take this long, but since they were obviously still busy, she turned back to go to her office. But Brad's words followed her.

"Well, that's why I didn't let it worry me until now, but what if it comes out before then? Don't you think it'll be tough to make me look innocent? Once a thief, always a thief."

Heart racing, Sheryl sped from the outer office before she could hear any more. Or worse, be caught listening. What the heck was Brad talking about? Make me *look* innocent, he'd said. Did that mean he wasn't?

Of course not, she told herself as she approached her office, but with "once a thief" ringing in her ears, it was tough to convince herself of that.

Guilt poured through her, but she couldn't isolate its cause. Eavesdropping? Disloyal thoughts about a friend? Arguing to the man she loved that he was completely wrong about Brad Hammond when she herself was having—

"Nathan!" Her hand flew to her chest, where her heart seemed intent on pounding its way through. "Good Lord, you took ten years off my life."

"Sorry." He looked up from the chair on the visitor's side of her desk. "My aim was 'pleasant surprise,' not cardiac arrest. I thought maybe I could take you to lunch."

She slumped in the doorway of her office, trying to look happy to see him. The truth was he was the *last* person she felt like facing right now. Not when she had so many unanswered questions about Brad plaguing her.

"If you're too busy, that's okay." He rose from the chair. "It's my fault for not calling first. I'd be happy with a couple of stolen kisses, and then you can kick me out and get some work done."

Finally, she managed a smile. "Can I get the kisses *and* lunch, or is that just too greedy? Let me grab my coat and tell Grace I'm going out."

He asked her to pick a restaurant, since they were in her neighborhood, but that turned out to be pointless, since she only picked at her food.

Peering at her with concern, Nathan asked, "You sure you're okay?"

Not in the least. "Yeah."

"Was my showing up a bad idea?" he wanted to know, pushing away his empty plate.

The last thing she wanted was for him to think she viewed him as clingy. She'd like to encourage his seeking her out and thinking of them as an involved couple. It made her happy that he was comfortable enough to drop by for lunch dates.

"Trust me, I was thrilled to see you. I'm sorry if my welcome lacked enthusiasm. It's..." She hesitated, knowing that she was again skirting the boundaries of what they'd agreed on. But didn't people in mature, healthy relationships discuss their lives? "Work. Tough morning, is all."

He nodded. "I imagine your job is pretty demanding right now." The perfect response. Sympathetic, but vague, not taking them any deeper into forbidden territory.

She reached across the checkered tablecloth to squeeze his hand. Everything would be fine. As long as she didn't lie to him, Nathan kept saying. But surely he understood that as Hammond's PR person, she couldn't go running to her journalist boyfriend with sensitive information, right?

"Nathan, hypothetically speaking, what if I did have to hide something from you?"

For the first time since he'd knocked on her door Christmas night, his expression hardened, his eyes glittering with some of the bitterness she'd seen in him before. "What do you mean, hide something from me?"

She swallowed, startled at how quickly the affection could leave his gaze. "Nothing. Forget I said anything."

When he opened the restaurant door for her a few minutes later, she noticed as she passed by how stiffly he held his body.

Feeling that she'd made a mess of things, she apologized. "I'm sorry if I wasn't any fun over lunch. It's not you."

He didn't answer for a second. "Sheryl, we're just starting out here, and I don't want anything to come between us. Is there something you should tell me now?"

Just that she loved him, but that might seem more like an escape route from the conversation than an honest declaration.

Brad's words echoed in her head. *Once a thief...*

"Sheryl?"

She might not yet be to the point of being tormented by a beating heart no one else could hear or staring blankly at her hands muttering, "Out, out, damn spot!" but her guilty conscience was definitely headed that direction. At the very least, she owed Brad her professional loyalty, but as close as she and Nathan had grown over the weekend... He was the man she loved. Didn't she owe him the truth, even if that truth were only that she didn't know what to think?

"Enough talk," she said, determined to subdue these thoughts until later. When she had plenty of aspirin handy. "How about those stolen kisses now?"

NATHAN RETURNED to his office less deliriously happy than when he'd left it. Everything had been so perfect between the two of them this weekend, but lunch had been awkward and...actually awkward about summed it up.

He slouched at his desk. Was she simply worried about the upcoming trial and what it might do to her company? Or was she hiding something from him? There had been that isolated moment this weekend, when she'd looked furtive about something. Then today...

Stop it!

In the past, suspicion had brought out his investigative nature even when there was nothing to investigate. The last thing he wanted was to run Sheryl off because of lack of trust, the very thing Kaylee had warned him about doing. Sheryl wouldn't lie to him, and he had to stop imagining intrigues.

She'd been constant in her behavior since day one, insisting that he was wrong and that her company had been falsely accused. And the more time he'd spent with her, the more difficult it was to see her as a liar or even an accomplice to a liar.

She wasn't the woman who'd dated Nathan to get back at an uncaring husband. She wasn't the woman who had turned her back on her family and abandoned them when things got rough. She wasn't even the person charged with intellectual property theft in the first place.

He really did have to stop looking for the worst in people. It was entirely possible that Brad Hammond was the slightly bumbling good guy he appeared to be and that it wasn't a sinister facade used to throw people off of his ambitious deceit. Now that Nathan thought about it, the whole thing sounded melodramatic. Did he really think Hammond had a dual personality and that Sheryl wasn't smart enough to see through someone like that after working with the guy day in and day out, even after being romantically involved with him? If Hammond were morally corrupt, she'd know.

She was too intelligent to be fooled by someone she knew so well. She might do her job even if Hammond was guilty, but she wouldn't argue passionately in his defense, especially not to Nathan, not after everything they'd—

A knock against the open door caught his attention, and he glanced up to find Beth the intern.

"I came looking for you earlier, but you weren't in the office," she said.

"Went out for a bite to eat. What's up?"

"We're getting scooped is what's up." She glanced down at her clunky blue shoes that probably weighed more than she did. "I'm sorry. It's my fault."

"Beth, what are you talking about?"

With a sigh, she ran a hand through her spiky-short, henna-rinsed hair. "Turns out I missed something when I did that double-check for you on Brad Hammond. There was a sealed court case I hadn't turned up yet. The findings should have remained confidential, but apparently a woman who wasn't a direct participant in the case leaked the story to another paper."

His mystery caller, Nathan surmised. "Why don't you come in and have a seat? Start from the beginning."

She eyed the vacant visitor's chair warily. "No, thanks, I don't trust those things."

But she did step into his office. When she perched

her tiny frame on the corner of his desk, she didn't so much as ruffle the stacks of paper he'd piled in his own unique organizational system.

"Brad Hammond was sued before," she said. "Do you still call it 'sued' when the parties don't go through the courts? He worked for a large corporation before going out on his own, and they claimed one of his start-up ideas was actually something he'd taken from them, from the development team he worked with."

Nathan's jaw dropped, but he pulled it closed with a decisive click of his teeth. "Was he found guilty?"

"Actually, no. The case was decided in his favor, because the corporation couldn't meet their burden of proof. It was a bad year for them. They'd recently sued another small company and won, but they took a drubbing in the media over it. People were in a huff over possible software monopolies at the time and accused the corporation of a David-Goliath thing, trying to keep small businesses from ever presenting a threat. So the company wasn't interested in a lot of publicity when they filed against a guy trying to start his own small company. Everyone agreed to private, confidential arbitration. I gather that no one directly involved was legally at liberty to discuss the proceedings afterward."

"How did you find all this out?" Nathan wanted to know.

"I have a friend who's an intern at the paper with the story. They got a tip from some woman and checked it all out. I think she might've once worked for Brad's former employer and knew about it. I know the corporation didn't want the story to come out, especially since they lost, and I'm sure that if Hammond stole something, he was perfectly happy not to have anyone find out. The story leaking can't be good for him."

No kidding, Nathan thought. A guy could claim getting falsely accused of a crime, as Hammond was doing in the Mathers case. But the *same* guy being independently accused by different sources of the *same* crime?

"I don't have all the particulars of the first case," Beth said apologetically, "though I suspect we can both read all about it tomorrow. He must have just got lucky the first time. Now that the public will find out about his track record, I don't think he'll get away with it so easily a second time. Sorry I wasn't the one to find all this out. But, for what it's worth, your hunch about the guy was spot-on."

He'd never been less happy to learn he was right.

The familiar, suspicious instincts he'd been fighting came back with a vengeance. The way Sheryl had mentioned the case after their first kiss. The way she'd brought it up after they'd made love, when he'd practically agreed to drop the story. *Why shouldn't I worry?* she'd asked. He'd gone out of his way to reassure her, telling her that what mattered was that she had never misled him or hid anything.

She'd looked away then, her features flushed. He'd noticed it at the time, but had told himself not to be the man Kaylee had accused him of being. Not to let a paranoid hunch ruin something important, something special.

Recalling Sheryl's jumpiness today, the way she'd changed the subject when he'd finally pressed her for a straight answer, he wondered if their relationship was a little less "special" than he'd assumed.

15

NATHAN RECALLED with irony driving up to Sheryl's apartment complex only a few days ago, nervous and excited and dying to see her. Now, as he steered his car along the same turns and curves that led to her place, he didn't know what to feel.

His dad, a good cop, had said that instincts were often a matter of common sense. If something—someone—seemed too good to be true, then it probably was. Nathan had followed that path of thinking for most of his adult life, and it had served him well both on the job and protected him in his personal life. He felt vulnerable now.

Sheryl, who was smart, funny, loyal, beautiful and sexy, definitely had all the qualities that would make a relationship with her seem too good to be true.

Weren't you the one who assured her that this relationship had nothing to do with your respective jobs or with Brad Hammond?

Well, yes... He'd also more or less promised not to write anything about Brad Hammond. And hadn't that been Sheryl's goal the first time she'd shown up, unexpected, in his office at the *Sojourner*? The little hairs on the back of his neck stood on end.

Okay, best not to dive into the deep end of complete paranoia. Brad's being an ambitious liar didn't mean

Sheryl was. Although she had seemed guilty of something during lunch.

What was it she'd asked him? *What if I did have to hide something from you?* Had she been talking about Brad's past? How long had she known? Long enough that she'd been protesting Hammond's innocence to Nathan even when she knew better?

Nathan parked his car, still not sure what he was going to say when he saw her. Their conversation when he'd called to ask if he could come over had been terse; she'd been as preoccupied and jumpy as she had been at lunch, only this time he hadn't been able to reassure her. And she hadn't been able to kiss him and distract him from what was on his mind, as she'd done after lunch.

"Don't jump to conclusions," he muttered as he killed the engine.

He was proud of the way he was handling this. The old Nathan might have automatically assumed the worst. Instead, he was coming straight to the source, going to Sheryl for answers, giving her a chance to explain herself.

Maybe once she had, this would all be better. Maybe they could laugh about it later.

He knocked on her door, and she opened it almost immediately, wearing the silk blouse she'd worn to work over a pair of baggy maroon sweatpants. At any other time, he might have chuckled over the incongruous pairing.

"Come on in," she invited. "Can I get you something to drink?"

Despite his tangled emotions, his gaze strayed toward the hallway that led to her bedroom. Tameka and

Ty weren't due back until tomorrow. Maybe if he and Sheryl got this sorted out...

"Something to drink would be fine. Whatever you're having," he told her.

"You said on the phone there was something you wanted to talk about?"

He followed her into the kitchen where she poured a couple of glasses of tea.

"I didn't really tune in to it earlier," she said, "because I had a demanding day at work myself, but something was bothering you, wasn't it?"

"Actually, yes." He accepted a glass and sat at the table, waiting until she'd pulled out a chair and joined him before he continued. "Sheryl, we need to talk about Hammond."

She bit her lip, clearly unhappy with the direction of the conversation. "But I thought we weren't going to do that. I mean, I know I've slipped a couple of times myself—"

"I know about Brad's past," he said. "I can understand why you wouldn't have wanted it to come out since your job is to protect Hammond's public image, but as of tomorrow, it's gonna be in the papers. I just... How long have you known?"

"Known what?"

He hadn't expected that. She'd clearly been upset this afternoon, had even hinted that there was something she couldn't tell him. Was she going to deny it now? "About the last lawsuit brought against him for stealing someone else's ideas."

"Brad's been sued before?"

The old Nathan and the one who'd realized this weekend he was in love warred with each other.

"You're honestly trying to convince me this wasn't what you were upset about earlier?"

Her gaze jerked up, tossing sudden sparks his direction. This weekend, her eyes had sparked with passion and need as she moved underneath him, but these were different sparks—the kind that made him wish he owned a Kevlar vest. "Wait a minute. I'm not trying to *convince* you of anything. Why do I feel like you didn't come here to talk but to put me on trial for something?"

"No." He needed to tread carefully, but he also needed to make his feelings clear. "I just thought that if this relationship is going to work, it was important we be honest with each other."

"I've always been honest with you." Despite her vehement tone, she glanced away when she said it. Her guilty conscience was *not* all in his imagination, and it was all the old Nathan needed to open the floodgates of repressed cynicism.

"So you stand by all those times you've argued that Brad was innocent? You're truly convinced that he isn't guilty of a crime he's been accused of twice?"

"Of cour—" Her hesitation, brief but unmistakable, infuriated him. "Of course he's innocent. You're crazy if you think he's a criminal."

"Crazy to think I'd get a straight answer from Hammond's PR person," he snapped.

"You wouldn't know a straight answer if it bit you on the ass."

"Excuse me?" His own anger had been building up such a head of steam that he was knocked off balance by hers.

She stood suddenly. "What is it, exactly, that you drove over here thinking? That the entire staff of HGS is involved in some conspiracy? Our affable boss is really a diabolical man stealing from people around the country, and his female employees sleep with reporters to convince them otherwise? Do you know how ridiculous that is? I knew you were jaded, but I didn't know you suffered from paranoid delusions."

He rose, too, flattening his palms on the tabletop. "Call me jaded if you want, but ninety-nine percent of the time I'm right about other people."

"Well, you're sure as hell wrong about me. And I was wrong about you." Her voice wavered. "I thought I loved you."

Her words burned inside him like acid indigestion. "Thought?"

The anger seemed to drain out of her, leaving only a troubled expression and a soft, sad tone. "I can't love someone who doesn't know how to trust, Nathan, and no matter how incredible our weekend was, you don't trust me. You really think I might have... You think I was lying to you the whole time? I'm not sure you'll ever fully allow yourself to trust a woman."

"I came over here so we could discuss the situation like two adults, not to get psychoanalyzed."

"Well, we've discussed it. You should go now."

"Sheryl—"

"I don't really want to have to be rude about this and throw you out."

He made it to the door and turned to look at her. "I could call you later." Despite the circumstances, he hated to think they were leaving it at this.

Her voice sounded a little choked when she said softly, "Don't."

Sheryl actually flinched when the door clicked quietly shut behind him. *What just happened here?* The executive in her knew she should be calling her boss and getting to the bottom of that previous lawsuit Nathan had mentioned. But she was a woman first, executive second, and all she could think about right now was Nathan. Yesterday, they'd spent hours laughing and talking and making love. Today, their relationship was over almost before it had begun. And she was pretty sure the problem wasn't just the Mathers versus Hammond Gaming Software suit.

It was Nathan, she decided, slumping weakly into her vacated chair, no longer needing to appear strong now that he'd left. She recalled the way his eyes had scrutinized her. *How long have you known?* He'd seemed like a professional interrogator, surprising her with a question while probing her with his gaze. That was what had bothered her, that searching, as though he couldn't possibly get the truth from her unless he unearthed it from underneath some imagined deceit.

She'd so enjoyed his company at the festival because his usual cynicism hadn't been in evidence. After their carefree weekend, she'd foolishly allowed herself to believe she'd broken through his suspicious people-aren't-half-as-nice-as-you-think edge.

But the way he'd looked at her just now...

Good grief, how seriously did he think she took her job that she'd sleep with a columnist to get a little good press for her boss? Maybe if Nathan were a *syndicated* columnist.

He would always be prepared to see the worst in those around him, though, wouldn't he? Or at least in any woman who claimed to love him, just waiting for her to betray him. Sheryl couldn't be in a relationship like that, no matter how crazy she was about the guy.

So that was it, then.

Without even looking, she'd found the right guy, a guy she could see herself spending her future with, *wanted* to spend her future with, and it was over already because of something as movie-of-the-week as trust issues? The only thing more sadly cliché was fear of commitment.

If Meka were here, the two of them would have a girls' night out, go to a club where Sheryl would probably drink in a futile attempt to mend her broken heart with liquid therapy. It wouldn't work, but why mess with tradition? Anything would be better than what she really wanted to do—crawl into bed and pull the covers over her and cry for the next twelve hours. But the sheets still smelled like Nathan, and she wasn't sure when she'd be ready to walk back into that room and see those flowers he'd traced over her skin last night.

Standing, moving stiffly as though she were about forty years older, she tried to recall her younger sister's number. They saw each other so often at their parents that there wasn't much to catch each other up on in the in-between times. Besides, Sheryl's sister actually had a nice love life, and was usually busy with her boyf—fiancé.

Please be home, Sheryl thought as she dialed the kitchen phone, sighing in relief when someone picked up on the second ring. Odd how Lady Luck was with her in this trivial instance, but had abandoned her in her fledgling relationship with Nathan. Fickle wench.

"Hey, it's me, Sheryl. You gotta quick second?" As soon as Lisa answered in the affirmative, Sheryl pulled the magnetic notepad off the refrigerator door, poised to write with the tiny pencil at the end of the string. "Can I get that recipe for your monster holiday punch?

Great, I'd really appreciate that. Yeah...um, for a New Year's Eve party. Makes twelve servings? Terrific." If she doubled the recipe, it might work.

"HEY, SHERYL?" The voice was little more than a whisper, but it still raked across Sheryl's head like...well, literally like a metal rake being dragged over the bruised skin of her face.

Is my face bruised? She couldn't imagine why that would be the case, but everything from her throbbing skull to the tip of her nose hurt. She tried to open her eyes to better discern what was going on, but her eyelids refused to cooperate. After a second attempt, she achieved her goal, belatedly understanding her body's instinctive refusal. *Light.* Ouch.

Light, bad. Darkness, good.

Unconsciousness, even better.

Sheryl tightly squeezed her eyes shut again—should her lids really scrape dryly against her corneas like that?—but in the second she'd been foolish enough to open them, she'd glimpsed a person standing in front of her. Not Nathan, since there'd been no tingling, electric sensation anywhere in her. She never wanted to see the jerk again, but she doubted that would have stopped her body from its normal, unfightable response. Besides, the voice had sounded female...

"Meka?" Whoa. She hadn't heard croaking like that since her brother had tried to scare her as a kid by hiding toads in her bed. "Y-you aren't—"

"Drink this, honey." Meka held a glass of water to Sheryl's mouth.

Since all moisture seemed to have been sucked from her body, Sheryl happily accepted the water. But something about the feel of a glass against her lips conjured a hazy memory. Drinking... Wait a second. It was all coming back to her now. The call to her sister, the vat of punch she'd tried to drown herself in, the flipping through the radio stations until she'd found an annoyingly sappy Richard Marx ballad on an outdated light-rock station. She'd sung along with him about love lost until a neighbor had complained.

It got fuzzy after that, but she knew there had been other ballads. And she suspected she'd played Meka's *Titanic* DVD, weeping like a baby when things didn't work out for Jack and Rose. She knew just how poor Rose felt. At least the man who'd broken Rose's heart had had the decency to die a noble death.

Pushing the water away, Sheryl reopened her eyes. The light was still an evil, excruciating force, but she figured she'd take what she had coming after behaving like an idiot. She wasn't much of a drinker, and her sister's recipe wasn't for amateurs. It would've been better to start with something less potent...say, straight tequila.

"When'd you get home?" Sheryl asked, hoping she hadn't been passed out for more than a couple of days.

"About two in the morning. They were predicting really bad weather and since the airports might be closed tonight, we left a night early, but there was only room on the late flight. Ty's actually the one who carried you to bed."

That explained why she was sleeping in the silk blouse she'd worn to work yesterday and how she'd managed to finally make herself return to her bedroom after deciding that she had to clean the sheets before using them again.

"You don't remember us getting in, do you?"

"Not as such." Truthfully, she wouldn't have remembered if the entire population of the metro Seattle area had tromped through the living room. "I was, um, pretty tired."

Meka snorted. "I saw the ingredients on the kitchen counter. Tell me you weren't using your sister's recipe."

"Okay, but I'd be lying."

Lying...mistrust...Nathan. Searing emotional pain.

As though she hadn't humiliated herself enough, Sheryl felt tears welling in her eyes. Interesting. She would have sworn she was too dehydrated.

"Ah, don't do that," her roommate pleaded. "You know I'll just cry, too. I'm assuming by the collection of '80s CDs lying on the living room floor and mostly empty bottle of vodka that you and Nathan had a fight?"

Sheryl struggled through the worst of the hangover to sit up in the bed, clutching the comforter to her the way she had when she'd been a kid waking up from a nightmare. "I love him, Meka. I actually fell in love with him, like you wanted."

"Trust me. *This* was not what I wanted for you." Meka's brows rose. "What happened?"

The story spilled out of Sheryl in halting phrases at first, then a flood she couldn't hold back. The doll he'd given her, the way he'd made her laugh when things at the festival were going wrong—the hours and hours of making love. Finally, she wound down with the startling news of Brad's past and Nathan's reaction.

Now that she thought about it, Brad's past was going to present a challenge to her job of making him look like the swell guy she thought he was. But she hadn't cared at all last night about her job or her boss. Only about the man who'd made love to her as though she were the most precious person on earth, but then had the nerve to contemptuously cross-examine her the next day as if she were a known criminal and he was the prosecuting D.A.

"Here." Meka reached across Sheryl to pick up a box of tissues. "You look like you might need—"

"What is *that*?" Sheryl grabbed Meka's hand.

At first, Sheryl had thought that the bright flash of light was just part of the post-punch-punishment she so richly deserved. But then she'd realized the light was actually glinting off something. A shiny something on her friend's left ring finger.

Sheryl squinted at the sizable rock, the second of its species she'd seen since Christmas. *Et tu, roomie?* "You're engaged!" *Note to self—no screaming exclamations when your head already feels like it's gonna fall off your neck and roll under the bed to reside with the dust bunnies.*

Meka bit her lip. "I wanted to wait until I got home to tell you in person, but two o'clock this morning didn't seem like the time. We certainly don't have to talk about it now, all things considered."

"Don't be ridiculous! Tell me everything." Sheryl's heart may have been pulverized, but Meka had been her best friend for years. "I'm so happy for you, both of you." So happy she could just cry.

"WHAT ARE YOU DOING HERE?" Brad asked, his eyes wide.

Sheryl lifted what was supposed to be a sardonic eyebrow, but it hurt her head and she winced instead. "I work here, and trust me, you need me today." Though Meka had called HGS first thing that morning, saying Sheryl was sick, Sheryl hadn't been able to avoid her responsibility once she'd seen that article in the *Sojourner*'s competitor.

And to think, all this time, she'd thought Nathan's paper would cause them problems.

Thoughts of Nathan added extra pounding bass to the drum line already playing between her temples. Knowing there wasn't enough coffee in all of Seattle— or all of Colombia, for that matter—to make this better, she dropped into one of the chairs opposite Brad. "You didn't think I'd stay away after I read the newspaper?"

Across from her, in his own chair, Brad rubbed his forehead as though he were in as much pain as she were. Ha—as though that were physically possible. "Should I have told you? I told Mark, of course, him being my attorney. I guess it would have helped you prepare if I'd been up front with you. But I wasn't *supposed* to talk about it. No one was. When that woman called me, asking for money to keep it quiet, I blew her off, but I guess since she wasn't an actual participant in the case, she wasn't bound by the same confidentiality agreements."

"You 'blew her off' but stayed worried about it, didn't you?" Sheryl recalled what he'd said about a phone call from a woman. "Who was she?"

"The ex-wife of someone I worked with. Saw me in recent news and wanted extra cash for the holidays. I don't know if the paper paid her for her tip, or if she told them to spite me. The ironic thing is, I was so relieved at the time that everything was kept confidential and now I wish it had been public record instead."

"So you're glad it's out in the open?" she asked.

"Not exactly...but it's worse now because it looks like I was hiding something. Honestly, Sheryl, I wanted to tell you about it before. I'd decided to go out on my own and ran into some company politics that made me choose to do it sooner rather than later. But I left right before a big project I was supposed to lead— starting it would have kept me there almost another year—and my timing ticked some people off. Not to mention the man who saw himself as my mentor felt betrayed that I was about to become the competition. The suit against me was little more than retaliation, an attempt to shut me down. But the so-called evidence was flimsy, which I guess is why they didn't want media attention.

"I didn't want it because I was just starting up, which is difficult under any circumstances, much less under a cloud of suspicion. Over time, it became something trivial. Didn't even matter."

"Until Kendra sued you for seemingly similar circumstances?"

He nodded, exhaling a frustrated sigh in a whoosh. "You believe me, right? I'd hate to think that..."

"I do believe you." She did, too. And she hated herself for second-guessing him. "I'm gonna do the best damn PR job imaginable and—"

"I'm sure you will. But why not start tomorrow? Mark and I have to decide how exactly to proceed before you can comment on anything anyway. And, no offense, sweetie, but you look like hell."

Despite the events of the past twenty-four hours, Sheryl managed a smile. "Gee, with lines like that, I can't imagine why you don't have better luck with women."

16

KAYLEE STARED UP in disbelief, her eyes wide and her mouth gaping.

Nathan fidgeted on the couch. "Aren't you going to say something?" She'd better, since she'd finally badgered him into baring his soul, an experience he usually avoided and hadn't found particularly pleasant.

She buried her face in the floor pillow she'd been lying against. When she finally looked up, she was glaring. "Be glad Frank's working tonight, or I'd probably have him take a swing at you."

Nathan's eyebrows shot up. "I'm new at this bonding thing, but shouldn't you be telling me that time will heal my wounds and suggesting we bake brownies or something?"

"You're an idiot."

"Again, not seeming all that sympathetic."

Kaylee sat up, flipping her long red hair over one shoulder. "Explain to me what you were thinking when you drove over to her place."

"It's like I said, I was giving her the benefit of the doubt." He still thought he'd done that part right. It was *after* he arrived that things had turned to crapola.

"Did you even listen to yourself while you were telling me everything? What did you say— 'I was giving her a chance to explain herself.'"

He protested her bad imitation of his voice. "I don't sound like that."

"You went in with the attitude that she owed you an explanation, that she'd done something wrong she needed to explain to you. I'm not sure why you asked her anything at all if you'd already decided she was guilty."

"I..." A memory nagged at him. His dad asking him about something they both *knew* he'd done, but his father had wanted him to be a man and admit it. Nathan had confessed, but then again, he'd been legitimately guilty.

Had Sheryl done anything wrong? Or had he just leaped to that conclusion even as he'd told himself he was giving her the benefit of the doubt?

"Kaylee, logic tells me that Sheryl had some knowledge of Brad's—"

Making an impatient, not-all-that-feminine sound in her throat, Kaylee held up a hand. "How do you feel about this woman?"

"I told you, I love her."

"Uh-huh. I love my husband. Have you seen his newest partner?"

He thought they were supposed to be talking about *him* here, but to be honest, that hadn't been going all that well anyway. "Don't remember, was he here at Christmas?"

"No. *She* wasn't. And she's stunningly beautiful."

"So are you," Nathan interjected.

"At the office, maybe. But Frank's seen me with morning bed-hair, stuffy with a cold and worse. Anyway, he and this woman spend hours and hours together, have a bond. I know lots of scary marital statistics that could keep me awake worrying at night, but

I'd like to think our love is a lot stronger than a statistic. So I don't want to hear about your supposed 'logic.' Do you have faith in this woman?"

The answer weighed heavily on him, especially since it was such an obvious one. "Yes. I do." So what had happened yesterday? Had his "logic" really been all that sound, or had he had a panicked, knee-jerk reaction to a woman getting so emotionally close to him for the first time in his life?

Had he sabotaged the relationship before he could tell Sheryl he loved her and make himself even more vulnerable to her? Was it too late to tell her now?

"Can I use your phone?" he asked as he shot to his feet.

She beamed at him. "You're a slow learner, but there's hope for you yet."

It was Meka who answered, and Nathan had to grovel to the fullest extent of his imagination before she'd call Sheryl to the phone.

"All right," Meka finally relented. "But I'm telling you, she doesn't want to talk to you. And she's *really* not feeling all that well, so don't blame me if she's in a bad mood."

They both knew whose fault her mood was. "When she hears what I have to say, maybe she'll feel better."

But he never got a chance to say it. Sheryl's greeting was also her goodbye. She hung up on him, taking only long enough to first let him know where he could stick the proverbial Yule log.

"HELLO?" a hesitant male voice called, as though uncertain the office was inhabited.

Sheryl supposed she wasn't visible behind the mountain of papers on her desk. "Back here!"

After sleeping most of yesterday and coming back to work this morning, she'd thrown herself into Brad's defense. He'd given her permission to access and print any interoffice e-mail about *Xandria Quest* that had circulated before the date of Kendra Mathers's first Web installment. Mark cautioned that it wouldn't be irrefutable proof that HGS had developed the idea first since it wasn't as though a company that designed complicated software couldn't manufacture a few documents, but it did help.

Sorting through the information had the twin benefits of assuaging her guilt for ever doubting Brad and giving her something to think about besides Nathan's phone call last night. And her somewhat less than mature response. He'd certainly think twice about approaching her again, which was all for the best. She couldn't be with a man who might never learn to trust, but she wasn't sure how she could resist him if he continued to seek her out.

Elliot Loomis peered around the stack of papers. "Ms. Dayton, we need to talk."

She sighed. Now was really not the time to hand out advice to the lovelorn.

He squared his shoulders and lifted his chin, his expression a combination of terror and determination. She half expected him to say, *We, who are about to die, salute you.*

"Elliot—"

"It's about Kendra Mathers, Ms. Dayton. I really need to speak with you."

Half an hour later, Sheryl leaned back at her desk, not having the first idea what to say.

"So" Elliot concluded nervously. "Am I fired? I

know you're a good friend of Mr. Hammond's and I was hoping you'd go with me when I tell him."

It hadn't been Grace he'd wanted her to butter up, after all. Sheryl still didn't know how to respond.

"Honest, Ms. Dayton, I always told myself... I didn't say anything at first because I love this job. I love this company. I'm fresh out of college and despite a killer GPA, I didn't have a lot of experience. Not everyone would have given me the chances Mr. Hammond has. I didn't come forward because the lawyers said it might not turn into anything, but I told myself if it ever went to court, I'd admit my indiscretion. You believe me, right?"

"Sure." He'd come to her today and admitted what happened of his own free will. And she could testify to the fact that he'd been trying to work up the courage to talk to her about this for over a week. She respected that, despite his original screwup.

When new ideas were in development, they were kept absolutely quiet. The gaming industry was a competitive one, and if your competition found out what your next bestseller was going to be, there was a very good chance they'd beat you to it, with their own twist. Everyone in development knew the rules about discussing a new project outside the office, but people, especially the company's die-hard fantasy fans, had been excited about *Xandria Quest*.

And apparently, Elliot, who didn't do well with women, had suspected other fantasy fans would be interested. For the past twenty minutes, he'd shared with Sheryl his shameful tale of how he'd attended the Seattle Sci-fi/Fantasy Expo last year. He'd wound up in the hotel bar one night, telling a couple of interested listeners about the new idea, high on his own importance of being named lead designer.

"I was interested in this cute brunette," he repeated as Sheryl mulled over his story. "I just wanted her to like me. I never thought for a second..."

At first, when Kendra Mathers's accusation had come out, Elliot hadn't made a connection. She wasn't the brunette he'd been paying attention to that night. But after seeing her picture, he'd realized he'd definitely seen her before. At the convention.

After checking her Web site and learning she was a huge sci-fi/fantasy buff whose stories had been rejected by numerous publishers and was seeking public attention, he'd searched his memory. Had she been one of the nearby listeners in the bar? A call to a buddy on the expo's planning committee had confirmed Kendra's name on the guest register. Elliot realized she'd had plenty of time to take the detailed information he'd shared and get it to the public long before the software was for sale. Ultimately, she'd created the proof she needed to set up a bogus lawsuit that would gain her and her unsold stories plenty of publicity.

"I'll go with you when you talk to Brad," Sheryl offered finally. "I'm glad you decided to come forward and am truly sorry—" he didn't know *how* sorry "—that we weren't able to have this chat sooner. But you have to understand this doesn't automatically make the case go away. Even if you testify that you blabbed the characters and game up and down the west coast, there are people who will think you're only saying what Hammond wants you to, in order to discredit Ms. Mathers. Still, between these e-mails and your admission...let's go see what Brad and Mark think."

Elliot gulped. "Right this second? I mean, I know

this is all my fault and I deserve to get fired. But...when I lose this job, it'll be like having my heart ripped out."

And stomped on by a guy in cleats. She was familiar with the sensation.

"YOU'RE SURE you're okay by yourself?" Meka asked for the third time.

Sheryl made shooing motions. "You guys have had tickets to see this play for months. And it's actually at a legitimate theater, probably not a naked Ping-Pong player in sight."

From beside the front door, Ty snapped his fingers. "Oh, man. If there aren't gonna be any naked people, I want my money back."

Meka shot him The Look and turned back to her grieving roommate. "But after the day you had at work, I know you're exhausted."

Mark had kept management and Elliot—whom a newly optimistic Brad declared punished enough by his own conscience—until almost seven. Sheryl *was* tired, but she'd appreciated the distraction from thinking about Nathan.

"Go, Meka, or you'll be late for the first act. I've already ordered Chinese food and have an evening for one all planned out. Highlights include flipping idly through fashion magazines and, if I feel really wild and crazy, a cucumber facial."

Meka laughed. "Okay. We're off, then."

Sheryl waved, sighing to herself once they'd left. She snuggled into her recliner and glanced around. All alone. In her own place. Tameka had confided that morning that she and Ty would be looking for an apartment. Nothing would happen immediately, but

Meka had wanted to give her fair notice since she'd soon be taking her half of the rent elsewhere.

It was time, Sheryl knew. She actually preferred having this place to herself to having to move out. Besides, Meka and Ty were taking a big step toward their life together, and she didn't begrudge them that. It was just ironic that she was finally going to be alone now that it was exactly what she *didn't* want.

As they'd been trying to do all day, her thoughts finally broke free of her iron control—okay, perhaps more like flexible recycled-aluminum control—and ran in the direction of Nathan Hall. Being angry and hurt didn't change how she felt about him one bit.

Never in a million years would she have suspected that poor, sweet Elliot Loomis was behind HGS's problems, and she would have called anyone who had suggested such a thing an idiot. Or a paranoid delusional. Nathan on the other hand, might have investigated the situation more thoroughly than she had, might have uncovered the truth weeks ago. Did that mean he was jaded and apt not to believe in people, or that she was too stubborn to see what was in front of her? Blind loyalty was little better than stupidity.

And even as loyal as she was to Brad, she'd had her doubts here lately. As a detached outsider, Nathan had assessed the situation and had similar questions, had even brought them to her to give her a chance to allay them. Instead, she'd thrown him out of her apartment and attempted to do herself in. Death by festive punch.

Then again, it hurt like hell that he'd come by his suspicions with a detached outsider's eye. Hadn't he felt closer to her than that after the magical weekend they'd shared?

The peal of the doorbell signaled the arrival of her

Chinese food, and Sheryl rose, retrieving the check she'd written from the pocket of her sweatpants. The teenage delivery guy thanked her for the tip and handed over the plastic bag. She was in the act of pushing the door shut when a taller, broader male form appeared in the hall.

She froze. Nathan was the last person she'd expected to see tonight. If she *had* been expecting him, she would have eschewed her comfy "I have PMS" sweatsuit in favor of wearing her red dress and an eat-your-heart-out expression.

"Sheryl!" Nathan jogged the last few steps forward to wedge his arm in the doorway. "Don't shut the door on me."

She hadn't had any intentions of doing so. She just wasn't sure what her intentions were yet. For that matter, what were his? "What are you doing here?"

"The same thing I was trying to do last night." He glanced around the hallway, then at her and the bag she held. "This isn't how I imagined it going, but...Sheryl, I love you."

Her container of Mu Shu pork hit the floor with a squishy thud.

"What?" Why was he doing this to her? There was no way she could bear to lose him now, but she knew eventually the cynical wall he kept his heart behind would break them up anyway.

"I do. I love you," he repeated, somewhat loudly, as though the additional volume would convince her.

The door across the hall opened partway, and an eye glared at them from behind a safety chain. "Could you people keep it down? Some of us are trying to watch *Survivor.*" It was the same guy who had knocked on

Sheryl's door to protest her impromptu Richard Marx concert the other night.

"Come in," she invited Nathan, even though she wasn't sure that them being alone in the apartment together was such a hot idea. Declarations of love could do funny things to a girl, make her forget all the reasons a guy was wrong for her.

But Nathan wasn't waiting around to be asked twice. He sped past her and entrenched himself on the sofa, whipping a small spiral pad out of the pocket of his leather coat. He flipped the notebook open, and she could make out words scrawled in black ink.

Ignoring the dropped bag of food—who could eat at a time like this, anyway?—she made her way over to the recliner, a safe distance from the couch. Had he actually written a speech for what he wanted to say when he got here?

"These are the names of some great investigators," Nathan told her.

"Huh?" Interesting segues this guy came up with. How did this follow his proclamation of love?

After the undiplomatic mess he'd made of their conversation the other day, *he* clearly had no future in public relations, but didn't he at least know you shouldn't blurt "I love you" and move on with the issue unresolved?

"If you say Brad Hammond is innocent, he's innocent," Nathan declared. "And as a journalist, I've amassed a great pool of investigative sources. We're going to utilize every one of these guys until we reach the bottom of this, together, as a team, and—"

"Nathan." Laughter escaped her, but it was tempered with the tenderness tightening her chest. She understood what he was trying to do, and she appreciated his effort. "I've already reached the bottom of it." In fact, hitting rock bottom was a pretty good description of her last couple of days.

"What? No. I wanted to show you that if you really, truly believe in him, then I do, too. Because I trust you, Sheryl."

I trust you. Tears misted her vision, and she blinked. Everyone made such a big deal over the "I love yous" and Lord knows they were important, but hearing Nathan say he trusted her...

Her lips parted, but no sound came out, just a dreamy, hopeful sigh. Which was all the prompting Nathan needed to cross the living room and kiss her senseless.

Between kisses he apologized frantically. "I...am so sorry. Can you...forgive me?"

She tilted her head back to grin at him. "If I didn't, do you think I'd be kissing you back like this?"

"So there's a future for us?"

Us. She liked the sound of that. Sudden laughter burbled through her. "Tameka wanted to find me a 'Boyfriend of Christmas Present.'"

"What?" His eyes narrowed in confusion, but she figured her segue wasn't nearly as random as his earlier one.

"You just missed that deadline. How do you feel about being the 'Boyfriend of Christmas Future'?"

She'd expected him to smile at her teasing, but instead he rocked back on his heels, his expression solemn.

"Sheryl, you've told me before that you were happy being single and could use more solitude and space. I don't want to push you...but is a boyfriend all you want?"

She swallowed. "Is that what you're offering?"

"No." He lightly squeezed her hands. "I've got a lifetime to give, if you want it."

If she wanted it? So filled with joy her chest hurt, she squeezed back. "You just try to get rid of me."

"Not a chance, I've already come too close to losing you. I was a jerk. But I have an idea of how to make it up to you."

"Bringing me coffee in bed every morning?"

"No, I was thinking more along the lines of..." He whispered a suggestion in her ear, and her eyes widened at the delightful proposition. Few things were better than coffee—but that was definitely one of them.

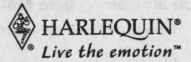

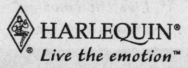

Forrester Square
LEGACIES . LIES . LOVE .

Award-winning author Day Leclaire
brings a highly emotional and
exciting reunion romance story to
Forrester Square in December...

KEEPING FAITH
by
Day Leclaire

Faith Marshall's dream of a "white-picket" life with
Ethan Dunn disappeared—along with her husband—
when she discovered that he was really a dangerous
mercenary. With Ethan missing in action, Faith found
herself alone, pregnant and struggling to survive.
Now, years later, Ethan turns up alive. Will a family
reunion be possible after so much deception?

Forrester Square...
Legacies. Lies. Love.

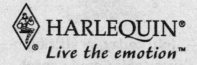

HARLEQUIN®
Live the emotion™

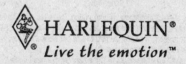

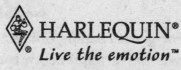